Kidnapped...

on Oregon's Coast Highway

(1926)

Joe R. Blakely

CraneDance Publications
a wing of BGleason Design & Illustration, LLC
Eugene, Oregon

CraneDance Publications,
PO Box 50535, Eugene, Oregon 97405
©2007 Joe R. Blakely   All Rights Reserved
First Edition, 2007

Library of Congress Cataloging-in-Publication Data
Blakely, Joe R.

An historical novel about the travels of a team of journalists up the Oregon Coast Highway during its construction in 1926, and their stalking by the woman's former fiance as he tried to overtake them.

Cover image from the Coos County Historical Museum. Maps on pages 6-7 from the Oregon State Highway Commission Biennial Report.

ISBN 978-0-9708895-8-4

Dedication

I wish to dedicate this book to my three favorite people: Saundra Miles, Justin Blakely and Jon Baker.

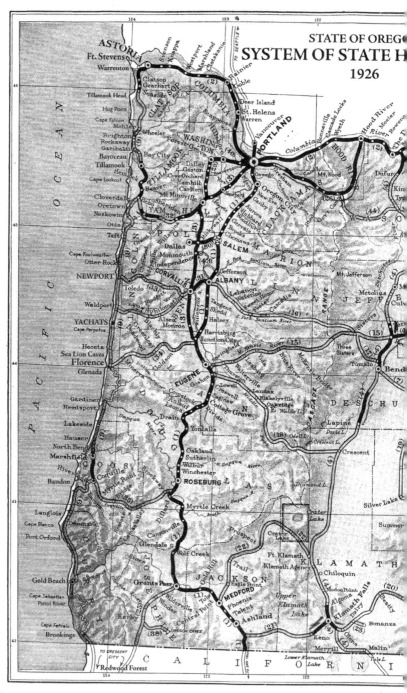

STATE OF OREG
SYSTEM OF STATE H
1926

Blakely   Kidnapped

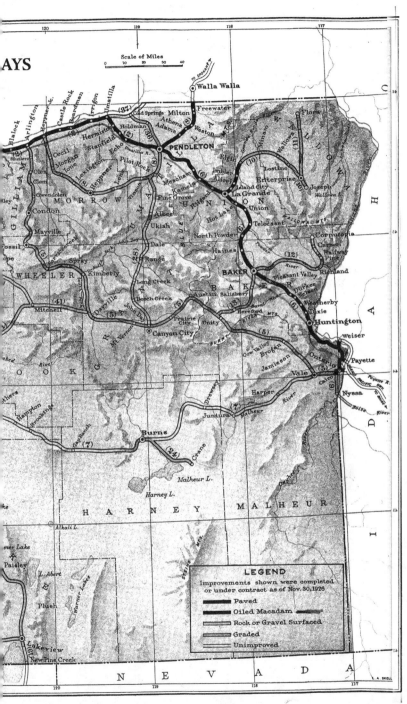

AYS

Acknowledgements

This book comes from research I did while writing *Lifting Oregon Out of the Mud*, published by Bear Creek Press in 2006. I envisioned a story that would include the Roosevelt Coast Highway and popular scenic spots as they actually were in 1926. The story came easily, almost as if ordained.

I'm indebted to these people for helping me with this book: Saundra Miles, and Carola Dunn; and, to Barbara Gleason for the front and back cover illustrations and her inexhaustible energy formatting and assembling this book. Most of all, I'd like to thank William L. Sullivan for his editing skills.

Like a silver thread I wind my
Way,
through forests, vales and hills:
By sparkling brooks of water clear;
O'er mountain grades and fills…
My course is laid through grandest
Views
Of mountain crest and valley
Stream.
Where sweetest native flowers
Bloom,
And scenic beauty rules supreme.

— Author unknown
Tribute to the Roosevelt Highway
circa 1920s

Chapter One

After a feverish effort to finish his sports column for tomorrow's paper, Ben Cooper reclined in his chair. He listened to the clatter of neighboring typewriters as he enjoyed a cup of coffee and a cigarette. A quivering circle of smoke drifted upward as Ben picked up that morning's *Oregonian*, June 1926. He turned the pages to get to the editor's mail. One op-ed article glared out at him.

OREGON'S COAST RANGE FORESTS THREATENED

By Eva Barton

Toledo's Spruce Corporation, a logging company near Newport on the coast, is chopping down trees faster than any other logging company in the United States. I read in an article from the Newport Journal that the devastation includes entire hillsides stretching for miles leaving nothing but stumps for the tourist to view. The Journal's reporter tries to bring sanity to this madness; his remedy is that the company should leave a swath of trees fifty feet wide along the road. In that way it would hide the ugly desolation brought about by the logging company's march with saws, men and trucks to chop down every tree in sight.

This is a particular cause for concern because this forest may be the largest one of its kind in the entire United States. They must stop this large scale destruction!

"Ben, is your article ready?" Sara Carson said interrupting Ben's concentration. When he looked up Sarah was standing there with her hand out. Sarah was the copy runner who took completed articles to the editor for reviewing. Her curled hair encircled a youthful oval, pretty face. Her bulky blouse tried to hide a shapely figure—a figure that had not escaped Ben's imagination. She was eighteen years old but impressed Ben with her mature attitude and quick intellect.

"Ah...have you read any of Miss Barton's letters?" Ben asked.

"Why yes I have," Sarah said. "Her father is a friend of Jess's. That's one reason why her letters are printed. She always writes about the Coast logging companies ruining the forests by cutting down trees that are hundreds of years old."

"That's absurd," Ben said. "Those companies are just trying to make a living. She's nuts!"

"Her father is a professor at Oregon Agricultural College and an expert in the field of forestry. Look, we can talk about this later. Jess wants to see you now." Sarah held out her hand.

Ben gave Sarah his completed sports article. He watched as Sarah rushed off to the other reporters, gathering up their articles. After she had circulated through the room she was holding a stack of papers that rose up to her shapely chest. She carried them into Jess's office. The editor's office was at one end of the big open room, enclosed in glass, so he could keep watch on all his scribes. Sarah laid the papers on Jess's desk and sashayed out through another door.

Ben knew that Jess was deeply concerned about the cutting down of old trees along the Coast. Jess was a fan of John Muir. He even subscribed to an organization trying to save the redwoods in northern

California. Still, Ben thought, all the exhortations against Oregon's fledgling coast corporations trying to eke out a living wasn't going to ruin his upcoming week-long assignment. His assignment was to observe and write about the progress being made on Oregon's new Coast Highway.

The Roosevelt Highway had been under construction since 1919 and promised to be one of the most scenic highways in the world when finished. Construction was taking a long time and Portlanders were anxious to find out more about it. If Ben was successful on this assignment he thought his editor might make him a department head. He sincerely felt that the importance of this position would bolster his sagging ego and help him conquer his two greatest fears: lack of self confidence and inability to find a woman.

Thus he looked forward to his trip, but also had apprehensions. After all, he'd have to drive from Crescent City, California to Astoria, Oregon on a partially finished road. He wasn't sure he could pull it off.

Ben gulped down his coffee, smashed out his cigarette, and left his cluttered desk, trailed by a wake of smoke fumes. He was the assistant sports editor. The high school baseball season was over and this new assignment would fit nicely between local sporting events.

Ben had been offered his job right out of journalism school and had been with the *Oregonian* for two years. He was twenty-two years old, five-foot-five-inches tall, and wiry in stature—almost elfin looking, yet lacking the bravado typical of smaller men. A mole covered a quarter of his right cheek. The mole's hair kept growing out and continually needed trimming. The mole had made him very self-conscious, and at times, it had almost made his life unbearable. Being made fun of was hard on him. He couldn't understand why a mole should make such a big difference. But the mole did single him out, as being weird, odd and some how unacceptable. This was especially true when he became attracted to a woman. Just last week he had asked Sarah out.

"There's a new Italian restaurant not far from here, would you like to go out for dinner tonight?" He asked when she stepped by his desk to pick up an article.

At first she giggled. Then her face reddened and her eyes flitted around the room nervously.

"Please don't ask me out anymore. It makes working here difficult. I've told you before that I'm hoping Edwards will ask me out."

If only I was as handsome or as tall as him, Ben thought.

"Please, your article."

To lessen the impact of these belittling episodes, Ben took up smoking and drinking. Still, he knew he did have some redeeming qualities. Mrs. Jones, the lady who ran the orphanage where he was raised, had often praised him for his golden hair and blazing blue eyes. She had been so proud of his writing skills.

Jess's door was ajar so Ben stuck his head in, "Sarah said you wanted to see me, sir?"

"Yes. Yes, come in and sit down."

Ben did as ordered. Jess's black desk phone rang and Jess picked up the receiver.

"Yes, what is it? Make it snappy I'm very busy." Jess's voice echoed in the small room. While Jess was on the phone Ben observed his cluttered desk, with its overflowing ash tray, scattered papers, and the picture of his wife and children. From above he felt the slight breeze of the ceiling fan. Ben always felt a little frightened by this big man.

Jess had hairy eyebrows, so hairy in fact Ben wondered how Jess could read the reporters' articles. His big pockmarked nose filled a large part of his face and beneath that was his huge black mustache. The only way Ben could tell Jess was talking was the bobbing up and down of his chin and his loud, commanding voice. The editor's manner unnerved Ben. He fidgeted in his seat.

Putting his hand over the mouthpiece, Jess said, "Go get me a cup of coffee, one teaspoon of sugar and a little cream. Hurry now, because we have a lot to discuss."

Ben rushed out to the coffeepot resting on a small table by a window. He poured the thick coffee, rich with grounds, in a cup. He sweetened it and returned to Jess's office.

Jess took a quick gulp and spewed the juice on the phone receiver.

"I want fresh coffee!" He bellowed and handed the cup back to Ben.

Again Ben made his way back to the table by the window and made a fresh pot of coffee. While no one was looking he took a quick gulp from the flask hidden in his vest pocket. Holding the coffee cup with both hands he returned to Jess's office and nervously handed the cup to Jess. Ben sat down and lit a cigarette.

"That's better, thank you," the editor said. "I've been thinking about your upcoming assignment along the coast. Do you think you can do this? I mean, I'm not sure you're ready for it."

"Yes sir." Ben said, hesitating just a little. He had heard tales of cars getting stuck in the mud, of being washed out to sea while driving on the beaches, and of flat tires. The ruggedness of the Oregon Coast

Highway in its unfinished condition was going to be a real challenge. Plus he had heard stories of wild animals, especially huge bears, roaming at large. This adventure might require skills he did not have. He hoped above all else, that because of the hardships he was about to face, Jess would crown him with the promotion Ben desperately sought. This might be his only opportunity for such an assignment. He took another puff on his cigarette.

"I'm up to it," Ben added as courageously as he could.

"The people of Portland want to know how the Roosevelt Highway is progressing. This will be a great opportunity for you to document that progress." Then he looked at Ben with a quizzical look on his face as if he wasn't sure Ben could really handle this job. "It's going to require nerve, stamina, and savvy to complete. But damn it, if you can find a way to survive the hardships, I'm confident you'll describe it better than any other reporter I have. I also want you to report on the fishing, hunting, camping facilities, resorts, golf courses and anything else you find interesting for our readers."

Ben managed to show his most impressive grin. He had to keep this assignment.

"You like working here don't you?" Jess asked.

Ben vigorously nodded his head.

"I'm glad to know that, because there is something that must take place simultaneously while you are traveling up the Coast."

"What?" Ben asked, dousing his cigarette in the ash tray. He could see his glorious trip slowly evaporating before his eyes. Ben sank back in his chair, thinking it all a ruse to get his excitement up, and then change the assignment at the last minute. Ben's blue eyes stared at the floor. Jess stood, his six-two frame towering above Ben.

"I'm assigning another reporter to accompany you on your trip."

Here it comes, Ben thought, another reporter. I don't want another reporter following me around. How can he do this to me?

"I want her written reports on the way logging companies are causing havoc in our Oregon forests. She's been trained by her father, Andrew Barton. He's taught her about the negative impact these companies are having. He's generations ahead of our times in his thinking. The sad part to this story is that no one will listen to him. They think he's crazy.

Your stories on the highway will be on the front page. But, the excessive cutting of timber worries me. I'd like her stories to document what's really happening over there. So, while you're gathering information on your story she'll be doing hers."

Jess's big frame fell back into his chair.

Ben noticed beads of sweat on the editor's forehead. Please just let me out of here with this assignment, Ben thought, and I'll take whoever you want me to take.

"I've arranged for you to pick up Eva Barton in Corvallis tomorrow morning. Be sure there's room in your car to accommodate her, including her suitcases and her camera equipment. She'll be your photographer too. You will learn a lot from this young woman.

It's been tough persuading Professor Barton to let his daughter go with you alone. I've spent considerable time trying to explain to him that you're an honorable man. Let me tell you, you'd sure as hell better treat this woman carefully. Anything untoward and you'll be fired immediately."

"Why the lecture? You know I wouldn't try anything with this Miss Barton." Ben responded.

"Professor Barton is reluctant because of things that have happened to her recently."

"What things?" Ben asked.

"That's not your business, Ben. Just make sure she gets back safe and sound. You'll have one week to complete the assignment. I'll want a full report about the conditions of the Roosevelt Highway. Have a good trip. Oh, and before you go, get me another cup of fresh coffee. "

Ben refilled Jess's cup and returned it to him in his office. With his coffee cup in his hand Jess walked over to his office door and held it open. Taking the hint, Ben walked out, not sure if there was a smirk or a smile behind Jess's mustache.

Ben could hardly wait to tell his friend Jerry what had happened in Jess's office.

Chapter Two

Ben sat at a small table in the back of a large crowded room, a speakeasy, smoking a cigarette and sipping scotch. Behind the bar whiskey bottles lined the shelves and on the walls, pictures hung of half clad, busty women. The bartender, a big burly man, busied himself by dispensing frothy mugs of beer. A blue haze of smoke hung in the air like a fog bank. Ben saw a crowd of men sitting at the bar. They wore brimmed hats, and turned up knit caps. They seemed to drink their beer with relish, Ben thought. The loud chatter of the patrons, made Ben want to cover his ears with his hands. A few of the men kept a wary eye on the big red light over the entrance door. Should it light up Ben knew he'd have to make a fast exit. This bar, however, had few raids. Their whiskey was the best in town.

Ben was waiting for Jerry Owens, the *Oregonian* reporter who covered city and regional news. Ben hoped he hadn't got into trouble entering the speakeasy. The speakeasy's access was through the back door of a bookstore. While pretending to look for books, speakeasy customers slowly walked to the rear where a bouncer admitted them to the bar. Finally Ben saw his friend come through the door. Jerry was a small man wearing a suit and tie.

"What kept you?" Ben asked. Jerry took off his smartly indented brimmed felt hat and laid it on the table.

"The city council meeting took longer than I thought." Jerry shouted over the noise. One member kept harping on speed traps being set up by Portland's motorcycle cops. He kept saying it just wasn't fair. As usual nothing was resolved, only put off for another meeting. Hey, isn't tomorrow the big day?" Jerry shouted over the noise.

"Yes it is. It'll be the first chance I've had to get out of Portland since I began work here."

A waiter came up to the table and looked expectantly at Jerry.

"I'll have a whisky on the rocks," Jerry said.

"Please fill my flask with Scotch, too," Ben said. The waiter left to fill their orders. The two men lit cigarettes and hunched forward so they could hear each other talk.

"I've been ordered to take Eva Barton with me," Ben said.

"You know that she's also involved with the women's temperance league, don't you?"

"No, I didn't know that. Damn! All I know is that she's written articles hell bent on closing down the Coast's logging industry. Where would all those Coast people work if it weren't for logging companies? Well, I'm going to make the best of it. I'll do my job and write my articles, and she can write hers."

Ben watched as the waiter wound his way through the crowd back to their table. The waiter gave Ben his flask and Jerry his drink. Ben stashed his new supply in his vest pocket.

"Why did you take this assignment, Ben?" Jerry asked.

"It has a lot to do with the orphanage I was raised in. I lost a lot of my self respect there and working at the paper hasn't done much to help. All my life I've been picked on."

"I know what you mean," Jerry said. "I'm small,

too, so I've had my share of bullies," Jerry said.

"My other problem is this damned mole on my face. Even now there's a gent staring at me as if I'm some kind of oddity. I was beaten up so many times in the orphanage I sometimes had to defend myself by falling on my back like a dog. Eventually people started to realize I wasn't a threat to them and left me alone. My one virtue is my ability to write. The only reason I'm able to do that is because, I delved into reading in an effort to get away from people. I read just about every thing I could find. After reading so much I wound up getting a scholarship to college and landing this job. If I succeed at this assignment I know I'll be promoted. Maybe then I'll be able to attract a woman. Jerry, I'm tired of being a bachelor."

"Me too," Jerry said. My goal is to marry Sarah."

"Good luck. I think she's after Edwards though."

"Edwards is leaving the *Oregonian*. Sarah has been spending more time chatting with me at my desk. I think I have an opportunity here."

"Best of luck, she's a great woman. Every woman I've ever been interested in has been horrified by this damned mole. Sometimes I get the feeling that the only thing that emboldens me is my Scotch." Ben took a sip of his drink.

"I've noticed how Jess uses you to get his coffee. He doesn't ask anyone else to go get him coffee, only you. Does that bother you?"

"Sure it does, but I don't want to lose my job. I get this feeling that he's on the verge of firing me with every word he says."

"Someday you ought to tell him to go get his own damn cup of coffee. He's not going to fire you, because he knows you're his best writer. He wants to save you for special assignments, like this Roosevelt Highway piece."

"Maybe someday I'll find the courage." Ben finished off his drink.

Just then a siren blared and the red light over the entrance door blinked on and off.

The bartender hopped up on a chair. "Police raid! Run for it!!"

"We got to get out of here," Ben cried. The back exit was right behind them so he and Jerry were the first ones to the door. It was pandemonium. The crush of bodies behind them forced them through the door like a small cork in a dam that had finally exploded, letting the water through.

They ran out into the alleyway. Light from the street lamp, half a block away, reflected off the puddles as Ben and Jerry splashed their way to the main street. Once there, they saw the front of the bookstore. A herd of policemen with helmets and nightsticks funneled through the entrance. Ben put his hand on Jerry's sleeve to slow him down. Then they mingled in with the busy pedestrian traffic. Ben heard the familiar sounds of autos on the street.

"Nuts," Jerry exclaimed, "I left my hat." The two friends waved goodbye and went in different directions.

Ben's black Buick coupe was parked against the curb. He loved this car. It was a standard six cylinder with an exterior sun visor, a hood ornament, running board and shiny fenders that covered inflatable tires. He especially liked the shiny spokes that jutted out from the wheel hubs. Ben enjoyed turning on the two big head lamps, which beamed out between the tire fenders and hood.

Ben's adrenaline kept pumping as he drove home. Tomorrow was the big day and he could hardly wait. He loved the thought of being away from Portland, the paper, and his arrogant boss. As the lamp posts flashed by he couldn't help thinking about what Jess had said. Damn it! Why had Jess refused to tell him about the things that had been happening to Eva?"

Chapter Three

Eva watched as her nanny, Martha Ingram, cocked her thin head to one side. Martha's straight black hair touched her shoulder. It was still black at forty years of age. When Eva talked of Tom she tried to hide her fear and couldn't help noticing Martha shudder. They were busy packing Eva's clothes for the trip up the Roosevelt Highway.

They stood at the foot of her bed. The bed was covered with Eva's belongings and the two were selecting items they felt Eva would use. Sunlight flooded the room from the open draped window. The two women's shadows stretched over the opened trunk and bed like silent, eavesdropping specters. The fir floor creaked as they moved back and forth. They folded Eva's clothes and neatly arranged them inside the trunk.

"I always wondered what you saw in Tom," Martha blurted.

"I think it was his curly black hair, dimpled chin, and brilliance in the classroom. All the other girls loved him too. When he settled on me I felt proud."

"I just wish your father and I had asked more questions about his family. I mean, his parents are weird. I know his father works hard as a logger, but it's what he and his wife do while he is not at work that should have alerted us to potential problems."

"I know. Whenever we went to Tom's house he wouldn't allow me inside. He'd say his folks were drunk on moonshine or fighting and he wanted to shield me from them. I think that's what is special about Tom; despite his parents he still got high grades and was popular at school. He managed to hide one side of his personality."

"You're lucky to be alive," Martha said.

"Oh, I don't think Tom wanted to kill me. I think he wanted to use me like his father uses his mother."

"Do you want to take your felt hats?" Martha asked.

"Oh, yes. I love the blue and red ones."

"What time is the reporter going to be here?"

"Soon. We better hurry."

"What really happened that night?" Martha asked. For ten years Martha had been mother and confidante to Eva. Andrew, Eva's father, had hired her not long after Eva's mother had died in child birth.

"If it hadn't been for my grandmother's brooch I would have been raped," Eva said. She had tried to spare Martha the details of that night, but, she decided she couldn't hide this matter from her confidante any longer.

"A brooch saved you?" Martha asked. "How?"

"Tom had me trapped in his car way out on Boone's road. At first it was just kissing. Then all of a sudden he hit me hard, so hard I almost blacked out. Then he started tearing off my blouse. I fought him off as best I could and he slapped me again. I managed to open the door but he held me down on the seat. As he ripped at my blouse he tore off grandma's brooch and threw it out the door. When he pulled at my skirt I managed to squeeze out of the car and fall to the ground. He slithered out and landed on top of me. He pulled my hair tightly with one hand and tangled up my legs in his, pulling again at my skirt. My free hand landed on the ground with a slap. Next to it was the opened brooch. Honestly Martha, it was like a mini dagger. I stabbed it into his back as hard as I could. In his pain he screamed at me 'You bitch!'"

"You poor, poor dear," Martha said.

"He arched upwards and jumped off of me. I knew I'd hurt him pretty bad. He stood next to the car rubbing his back like a horse rubbing against a fence post. I just had time to jump up and run. By the time he started after me I'd veered off into the forest. It was dark and I was terrified. I positioned myself close to the road so I could see if he'd follow. Not long after, he drove up the road with the car lights on. He yelled for me, pleading and saying he was sorry, over and over again," Eva said.

"You don't have to tell me any more. I know you've been through a lot. Somehow you've got to get this terrible scene out of your mind."

"Martha, those policemen wouldn't believe me. They told father and me that this type of behavior happens all the time."

"Couldn't they see the bruise on your face?"

"It hadn't swelled up then. It was too soon after he'd hit me."

"You've got to forget about Tom," Martha said.

"I'm trying Martha, you know that, but he keeps sending me flowers, and keeps calling to apologize. Last week he telephoned father and father slammed the phone down. I hang up on him all the time. He hides in the bushes up the road so he can watch the house. I want him out of my life!"

"That's probably why your father decided to let you go with this reporter from the newspaper. It will give you a break, away from this lunatic. The editor assured your father that Ben Cooper is an honorable man and will treat you with the respect you deserve. Besides, honey, there are nice men out there. My husband was the best man in the world. I had a hard time going on after he died of pneumonia. You shouldn't let this one man ruin the rest of your life," Martha said.

"We better finish packing, Ben will be here soon. I want everything out on the porch. I want to be ready." Eva had to admit, she was afraid of men. But, she thought, my mission of finding out what the coast forests are like is more important to me than my fear. Besides, father needs me to write about what I observe over there.

"My dear, you must also try and have a good time," Martha said.

Chapter Four

On Monday morning Ben drove south, leaving Portland and the *Oregonian* behind. He was excited. When he reached Salem, the sun lit up hilly farmlands bursting with color. What a glorious day to be starting out on his assignment! If only he could be doing this job alone. Oh well, he thought, I'm going to make the best of it. He took a swallow from his flask and replaced it in his vest pocket. Salem slowly disappeared in the rear view mirror. The next town he passed through was Albany. Smoke drifted up from small lumber mills. He felt jubilant, free and alive. He pulled out a cigarette and lit up. Smoke eased out through his nose as he drove into Corvallis.

He threw the cigarette out the window and pulled over to the side of the road, frustrated that he couldn't find Eva's street. He pulled out the map Jess had given him. Jess was an astute editor but map making was not his forte. Ben was just able to make out the name of Eva's street, Daffodil Drive. Ben slammed the gear shift back into first, then second gear, and slowly drove the streets of Corvallis. It wasn't long before he came to Eva's street. "Finally," he whispered. He drove down the gravel lane until he found Eva's house. It was eleven a.m.

She was waiting on her front porch, slowly rocking back and forth. Her Victorian home stood two stories tall. An octagon turret protruded out on the north corner, capped off with a pointed metal spire. The porch wrapped around the front of the house and along one side. A white picket fence adorned the front yard.

Ben parked in front of the gate, waved, and watched as she stood and walked down the stairs to greet him. He noticed her colorful, long-sleeved dress, hung to her ankles. Covering her head and hair was a bright blue, brimless felt hat. Ben would never forget her smile; it was simply the most splendid greeting he had ever received. His mental processes went numb. He felt inner butterflies and uneasiness in the presence of such beauty. Unconsciously he grabbed for his flask, but dared not display it. When she opened the gate Ben noticed that she was just a little shorter than him, with a shapely figure. She looked to be about his age. Ben placed one hand nervously on the steering wheel. With his other hand he pinched himself. Come on Ben, he thought, it's only another human being. He opened the car door, tripped, and fell to the ground. He looked up and there she was with her sparkling brown eyes, her curly brown hair peeking out from under the edge of her hat, her seductive lips and her sweet feminine face. She was the loveliest woman Ben had ever seen.

"Hi, I'm Eva," she said. "You must be Ben?"

"Why, er... Why, yes I am." Ben stuttered. He slowly got up, wiping the dust from his pants and feeling incredibly embarrassed. "It...it, looks as though you're all ready to leave. Are all those things on the porch yours?"

"Yes they are. It appears there won't be room for everything. I was hoping you had a bigger car."

"I'll take out my golf clubs and fishing gear. That will make more room for your stuff. But I'm keeping extra tires, tire patching equipment, tire chains, shovels, and ropes. In case we get stuck, you know."

Ben hung over the seat as he rearranged the gear. "There, that will help." Then he handed the fishing pole and box to Eva. He pulled out his golf clubs. They carried his stuff to the front porch. Then they brought Eva's clothes, books, and camera gear to the car and stuffed them behind the seat. The rear window was almost covered up by the pile. Eva still had a few more items. So back to the porch they went. Once back on the porch, Ben noticed a bouquet of roses on the floor, near the steps on the north side of the house.

"Do you want to take those flowers?" Ben asked.

"What flowers?" Eva noticed the flowers for the first time. She rushed over and began stomping them. Then she kicked the mangled mass from the porch. The force of the kick caused her to lose her balance and fall backwards. Ben rushed to catch her. It was the first time he had ever held a woman in his arms. Too bad it had to be in such an awkward situation, Ben thought.

"Oh!" Eva exclaimed, pulling herself away from Ben and straightening her dress.

"I've told him numerous times not to send me flowers." And then in a barely audible voice, "Why does he keep harassing me?"

"What's wrong out here?" Andrew Barton asked, coming out the front door.

"Oh father, look what Tom has done! More flowers."

Andrew took Eva in his arms. "There, there, stop crying. Everything will be all right. You're off on your adventure today, and leaving this mess behind. Maybe Tom will come to his senses once you've left."

"I hope so. Father, I'm so embarrassed at getting mad. Ben, I hope you won't think badly of me." Eva stopped. "Oh, my. I haven't even introduced you yet. Father this is Ben Cooper from the *Oregonian*. He's the reporter Jess told us about."

"My pleasure to meet you," Andrew said, stretching out his hand. As they clasped hands Ben noticed that Andrew, dressed in coat and tie, had a scraggly brown beard, a thick crop of hair and was his same height. Ben was very impressed by this dignified man. Ben smiled.

"I'm pleased to meet you, sir. I'm anxious to get moving, we need to reach Grants Pass by evening."

"Yes, let me help with the rest of my daughter's things," Andrew said. With the three of them carrying Eva's gear it wasn't long before the car was crammed full. Then Andrew stood by the car next to Eva. Ben heard him say, "Everything will be all right, honey. I'll talk to the sheriff one more time and let's hope he'll listen this time."

Ben opened the passenger door for Eva. Then he hurried around to the other side of the car and climbed into the driver's position. He turned the ignition switch and the engine hummed.

"Wait," Martha cried rushing out of the house with a picnic basket overflowing with freshly prepared food and a red tablecloth. She handed it to the professor. "I prepared this supper early this morning and in the rush to leave I forgot to tell Eva about it."

"I wish I were going just so I could eat it," Andrew said with a smile. "That chicken smells good." He passed the basket through the car window to Ben. He passed it to Eva.

"Thanks, Martha." Eva set the basket on her lap.

"You kids have a safe journey. Eva, take good notes. I want to know what those loggers are doing to our forests," Andrew said. "Good bye, I'll see you two in a week."

"Bye," Ben said. He was glad to finally get started.

The car jerked when clutch and gas pedals fought for their proper positioning. His car moved away from the fence and out onto the road that would carry them to the Pacific Highway and south to Grants Pass.

Ben pulled out a cigarette from his pocket and lit up. As he inhaled he wondered what all the fuss was about those flowers, and why Professor Barton told Eva he would talk to the sheriff one more time. There was something more he had to learn about Eva, more than just her views on trying to save the Coast Range forests.

Chapter Five

"I'm looking forward to dinner," Ben said. "That aroma from Martha's basket is making my mouth water."

"As we drive south let's look for a nice spot and have a grand picnic," Eva said.

"There'll be plenty of scenic spots," Ben said, exhaling a large puff of smoke. The smoke drifted past Eva and out her window.

"Ah-chew!! I can hardly wait to get to the Coast. There must be lots of beautiful spots there. I've checked the *Blue Book* maps and also a map from my father. Still this is my first time to the Coast. What do you know about the route we'll be taking?" Eva asked.

"This will be my first time too," Ben admitted. "My plan, though, is to take this highway to Grants Pass. We'll stay the night there. In the morning we'll drive to Crescent City, California. Be sure and have your camera ready. I'm told the tallest trees in the world grow there."

"Yes, I know," Eva said. "My father made me promise to get good photographs of the biggest trees I could find. Where will we go from there?"

"From there our journey will take us north on Coast roads all the way to Astoria. Much of the highway is being worked on, so there will be many detours. My goal is to reach Astoria in a week's time. We can write our articles there."

"I hope we'll have time to camp in a forest," Eva

said. "My father would like me to collect some samples of the vegetation and insects I see."

"We'll have plenty of time for that," Ben said.

At 35 miles an hour, it was going to take some time to reach Grants Pass. They both settled back in their seats and prepared for the long ride. The gear shift knob jiggled back and forth between them. Air whisked through the open windows, and when Ben looked into the rearview mirror, he could see the road vanishing to a thin line on the horizon. Ben flicked his cigarette out the window and heard Eva's subtle sigh of relief.

"Anything wrong?" Ben asked.

"Yes," Eva said. "Since we'll be cooped up together for a week I must tell you that whenever I'm in a moving car and someone is smoking I feel ill. If you could stop smoking while we're in the car it would be nice."

"Sorry," Ben said. "It's a nasty habit. I started smoking in order to get my mind off other problems."

"What problems?" Eva asked.

Ben slowed to let a horse-drawn wagon, carrying gravel, cross the road.

"Aw, it's just that…aw heck, I might as well tell you. I'm an orphan and I was raised in an orphanage. When I was two, my mother caught smallpox. She was afraid I'd get infected so she left me with friends. She went off to die in a smallpox colony. I never heard from her again. I was shifted from family to family until I eventually ended up on the steps of a Portland orphanage."

"Do you know anything about the family that left you there?"

"Yes," Ben said. He reached into his back pocket and pulled out his wallet. Ben pulled out a yellowing piece of paper. "After my graduation from high school,

the lady who ran the orphanage gave me this note."
He handed it to Eva. Eva quietly read aloud the words
written on it:

"*To whom it may concern: Ben Cooper is the
child's name. We think he's two years old. We are
short of funds and find it hard to eke out a living for
ourselves. This child places an extra burden on us
that we are unable to meet. Therefore we are putting
him in your care. All we know of his family is what
news was passed on to us. His mother's name is Rosa
Cooper and she had smallpox forcing her to abandon
this child. We think she's dead. He is a good lad. Please
care for him. Jim and Mavis Brown.*"

"Have you tried to locate these people? Eva handed
the paper back to Ben.

"There's no trace of them, anywhere." Ben said,
replacing the paper in his wallet.

When the wagon had passed, Ben shoved the gear
shift forward and they slowly began to move until once
again they were breezing along amid pastoral lands.

"So, that's all I know of my mother. I know
nothing of my father. My upbringing in the orphanage
was chaotic. I turned inwards and read books. That
helped me get through high school and college. After
graduation I was given the opportunity to work for the
Oregonian."

"It must be terrible not knowing what your parents
are like," Eva said.

"I've always wondered. How did my father earn a
living?" Then Ben paused a moment, wondering if his
father had been as gutless as he was. Ben wished he'd
had a father to teach him how to be a man.

"I yearned for the love of a mother," Ben said
aloud. "Were my parents irresponsible people? Were

they embarrassed by the mole on my cheek? Maybe they invented this smallpox idea as a way to get rid of me. They must have been asked countless times; 'What's that on your son's face?' I know, God knows, I've been asked that same question many times, from complete strangers."

Eva lowered her eyes, "I'm sorry. People sometimes say such hurtful things."

"Well, maybe my parents got tired of people asking stupid questions. I just don't know what happened and it really bothers me. I probably shouldn't tell you this but because of everything I've been something of a loner."

"I'd like to be your friend," Eva said.

Ben looked sideways at Eva. How could she say such a thing; they'd just met. Still, there was sincerity in her voice that told Ben this woman could be trusted.

A car drove up behind them and beeped its horn, a signal in those days to pass. Ben slowed and the car passed.

Soon they reached the outskirts of Eugene. A sign next to the road read, *Speed limit 15 miles per hour.* Ben slowed as they drove into the city. Just as they crossed over the trolley tracks a motorcycle cop passed them.

"Careful," Eva said with a smile. "We don't want to get a ticket."

Ben nervously shifted into second gear. He looked north on Willamette Street and saw a multi-storied hotel. He also saw parked cars lining the curb in front of the busy commercial shops. Once through town, Ben sped up to 35 miles an hour. They passed through the towns of Cottage Grove and Drain.

Just north of Oakland, Ben asked, "Is it time for dinner yet?" The thought of eating fried chicken was overpowering to him. "We better eat soon or I'll lose control of this car and we'll end up in the hospital."

"We'd better eat then," Eva laughed. "How about under that bridge? There's a turnoff over there."

Ben drove down a side road to a beautiful little bridge that spanned the easy flowing Calapooya River.

"We can eat by that log," Eva said.

Eva spread out a blanket on the ground. They both used the log as a back rest with the bright red tablecloth under the basket of food between them. Eva prepared a plate of food for Ben. Then she made one for herself. The sun stood brilliant in the sky. They sat under a huge old maple tree with its big leaves radiating a light green color. Eva dug her fork into some coleslaw and Ben gnawed at a chicken bone. The river flowed peacefully by.

"This chicken is really good," Ben said.

"My father loves Martha's fried chicken, too," Eva said. "Since we're being so honest with each other, I have a request of you and please don't think me silly or impertinent. I don't believe in drinking moonshine. I won't deal with drunkards! But if you need a nip once in a while that's all right with me. Agreed?"

"Agreed," Ben said as he tossed the leg bone into the river. He began nibbling on a wing when he noticed a car slowing to a stop on the bridge. The driver was staring down at them. The car stayed there a full five minutes. Then it moved on because of a car behind it. Eva was facing away from the bridge so she didn't see the car.

"That's strange," Ben said.

"What's strange?" Eva said.

"There was a gent staring at us from the bridge."

"What?" Eva said, startled. She turned and looked up at the bridge.

"He's gone now. A car pulled up behind him and he had to move on," Ben said.

"Did you get a look at him?"

"I saw his face. He had high cheekbones and curly black hair. Why?"

"I was afraid this might happen," Eva said.

"What do you mean?"

"I didn't want to tell you this, but I guess now I have too. You should probably know, just in case it was Tom."

"Who's Tom?" Ben asked.

"Tom Bigalow and I were to be married this month. A few weeks ago I backed out of the engagement. He's been mad ever since. He can't seem to accept it."

"Were the roses from him?" Ben asked.

"Yes," Eva said in a whisper. She filled their plates with more chicken and coleslaw. "While in high school, my senior year, I fell in love with Tom. I admired his handsome looks, wit, and intellect. He graduated with the highest grades in our class and he reminded me a lot of my father."

"If Tom was so much like your father, why didn't you marry him?"

"There was a side of Tom's behavior he'd kept hidden from me. He's a depressed and unbalanced man."

"I'm sorry to hear this."

"If only I had known this earlier it would have saved a lot of hardship. I know this all sounds strange. Maybe I can explain it better, by giving you a little family background. My father has been teaching agriculture, and studying forestry for the last 12 years. It put quite a strain on him when my mother and sister died in childbirth. That was about ten years ago. He hired a full time house keeper and nanny, Martha Ingram, who was to help me whenever she could. She has been my best friend and like a mother to me. Yet, I still felt deprived not knowing much about my real mother."

"Just like me," Ben said.

"I suppose so. But my relationship with Tom helped me to feel worthwhile, needed. It filled a gap and took my mind off of my mother."

"I see," Ben nodded.

"My dates with Tom continued after graduation. Then we both entered Oregon Agricultural College. Tom got excellent marks in animal husbandry and was working his way through school. My class study was in English with an emphasis on writing. The more I listened to my father the more I became alarmed about logging companies cutting down old trees. My father and I felt they were ruining virgin forests. I decided to take an active role in trying to stop them. That's when I began writing papers and articles, some of which Jess published for me, in the *Oregonian*."

"I've read them. But that doesn't explain Tom's strange behavior."

"I'm getting to that. Tom's family is quite different than mine. His father is a logger and his mother hardly ever leaves home. Tom went out of his way to keep me from meeting them. I later found out that his illiterate father battered Tom's mother ruthlessly. One of the reasons she never left home. They both drank moonshine to excess and their fighting is still a weekly occurrence. Tom was deeply affected by these happenings. At the time, I didn't really understand how deep. I thought that I loved him."

"This is interesting because both of you were raised so differently," Ben said.

"I know. It's what influenced the huge spat we had. That's when I decided to call off our wedding. He's tried everything to make me change my mind. He continues to send me flowers, call our house to apologize and he even watches my house from hiding spots on the street. It's come to the point that I'm really frightened as to what he might try next."

Ben threw the wing bone into the river and handed the empty plate to Eva. She began repacking the picnic basket.

"My father and Martha were hoping that while I was away, Tom would come to his senses. Evidently he has chosen to follow me."

"The man I saw on the bridge had black hair. Can you add anything to his description so I'll know him if I see him?"

"He's a little over six feet tall, with blue eyes, a dimpled chin, and a medium muscular build. He's very strong. He also walks with a limp. When he was little he broke his left leg and it never healed correctly. Oh, and one more thing, when he's worried he continually runs his right hand through his hair."

"I'm not entirely sure the man on the bridge was Tom. Now that I know what he looks like, I'll keep an eye out for him. Do you think he's dangerous?"

"I really don't know," Eva said. "Martha thinks he is." Ben saw a tear in Eva's eye. She carried the basket to the car, and Ben brought the red tablecloth and blanket.

On the ride to Grants Pass Ben thought about Tom Bigalow. Why was he harassing Eva so much? It sounded like he'd made an obnoxious fool of himself. Why couldn't he just accept the fact that Eva didn't want to see him anymore? And what bothered Ben even more was knowing that the man on the bridge could have been Tom.

Chapter Six

It was six p.m. when they reached Grants Pass, a logging town. They parked in front of the tallest building in town, the hotel. They rented adjoining rooms on the third floor. Ben insisted that they finish eating the picnic basket's remaining food. They ate it in the lobby of the hotel. Then, they retired to their rooms.

Once inside his sparsely furnished room Ben pulled out his flask and took a big gulp. He lit up a cigarette and sank into a chair by the window. Through the white laced curtains he could see the main street below. The town was quieting down for the evening. He pulled out his notebook and wrote about the towns they had passed through and the condition of the Pacific Highway. Not a bad road, he thought. It had allowed them to make very good time. When he had finished writing, he snuffed out his cigarette and then thought of Eva. Ben hoped that the upcoming trip would help Eva forget all about Tom Bigalow.

He was impressed with her beauty, her cheery intellect, her forthrightness, and the fact that she didn't seem to be bothered by his disfigurement. This might be an interesting trip after all. He didn't regret having to take Eva along with him as her presence was comforting to him—not accusatory or belittling. He could live with not drinking or smoking when she was present. It would be hard to curtail these habits but he liked being with Eva, so he would put forth the effort. From his suitcase he took out his small scissors and mirror. He began trimming the hairs on his mole.

When he finished, Ben put away his grooming tools. Then he took off his shirt and pants in preparation for bed. Looking out the window he noticed the daylight slowly fading. Through the thin walls he heard footsteps in the hallway. Then he heard a knock on Eva's door. Who can that be, he thought? He heard the door creak open. He went to his door, opened it a crack, and peeked out.

"Get out of here!" Eva shouted. Ben saw Tom drop a bouquet of flowers and grab Eva by the arm. Ben didn't know what to do. He ran back to his bed, grabbed his pants and desperately tried to put them on. He could hear Eva in the hall shouting. He slipped and fell, got back up, pulled up his pants, and raced back to the door.

As he entered the hallway he saw an older couple that had just come up the stairs. Ben heard the old guy's forceful command: "Let go of that woman!"

Ben saw Tom let go of Eva and race for the stairs. Tom collided with the old man, knocking him to the floor. Then Tom raced down the stairs and disappeared.

"Eva, are you all right?" Ben asked.

"Yes," she said, crying. She leaned against the door jamb, with her eyes magnified by the flood of tears. "It was Tom." The bouquet of stemmed red roses lay at her feet. "You'd better help the old man."

"Let me help you up, sir," Ben said. He carefully grabbed the man's arm and helped him to his feet. Then he returned to Eva.

"Quick, Ben, you might be able to see him through my window. Lets make sure he's not coming back."

Ben went to the window and waited until he saw Tom enter his car. It was a black Ford sedan with a cloth-covered top and a front window that opened for ventilation, the same car he had seen on the bridge.

The car drove off and out of sight. Eva was still crying when Ben came back from the window. The older couple was trying to comfort Eva.

"That was the car I saw today on the bridge," Ben said. Eva nodded in response.

"If you need us for anything just knock on our door," The gray haired man said. "We're in room 312."

Ben and Eva thanked them for helping, and watched as they entered their room and closed the door.

"Eva, part of my assignment on this trip is to make sure you have a safe journey. Your articles are very important to Jess. I know your father is also counting on you to relay to him information about the forests. We can't let this sort of thing with Tom happen again. Maybe if you were to share my room, Tom wouldn't be so bold."

"I don't think he would be either. But I'm not sure about sharing a room."

"I'll pull the mattress from the bed to the floor, and you can sleep there. I'll sleep on the box springs. I promise I won't bother you in anyway. I'm not like Tom." Eva thought for a long time finally nodding, accepting the situation. She quietly returned to her room and picked up her belongings. She moved them to Ben's room.

"From now on we'll spend our nights together," Ben said. He couldn't help feel compassion and empathy for Eva. He desperately wanted to help her, keep her safe. He must gain the courage to stand up for this woman! These thoughts along with Eva's barely audible sobbing kept him awake for much of the night.

Blakely Kidnapped

Chapter Seven

Ben dragged himself off the mattress and put on his clothes. He gently shook Eva's shoulder with his hand. "Wake up Eva."

"Do we have to get up," Eva asked. "I just got to sleep."

"Yes. It's Tuesday, and as soon as you're ready we're off to the redwoods."

"What about Tom?" Eva asked.

"I'm not sure," Ben said.

"He seems determined to stalk me. Hopefully, he'll lose interest the further we are from Corvallis."

"I hope so," Ben said. "If he bothers you again we'll report him."

"I'm not sure that will do any good. My father reported him and the sheriff laughed in his face. It seems that the law has to see my dead body first."

"That will never happen as long as I'm with you," Ben said, surprising himself with a new-found valor. "Now let's get moving." And he threw his pillow at Eva.

It was another beautiful day. The sun lit up the back of Ben's car as they headed southwest. The nice gravel roads led them through tall trees that rose up all around them. They found themselves taking excursion trips on backwoods roads, curious to see what lay at the end. Most of them were rough and bumpy logging roads, but on a smoother road, they drove half way up a mountain towards the Oregon Caves. Ben decided to turn around because the coupe's radiator started to steam. The geyser of steam diminished as they came off the mountain and turned towards the Coast. Soon they crossed over the border into California, Ben checked his watch. It was noon. When they got to the city limits of Gasquet, Eva read the road sign aloud.

"*Eighteen miles to Crescent City*. We're approaching the redwoods! I've looked forward to driving through the redwood forest since I was a child. I can't believe I'm actually here."

Ben was awed by the huge trees that dwarfed everything else in the landscape. Giant pillars rose hundreds of feet into the air. Their trunks were big enough for a truck to drive through. He looked off into the forest and saw a heavy mist rising, enshrouding the thin needled branches, with their cones draped down from big branches high above. The thick canopy of limbs blotted out the sky. Lush ferns covered the forest floor. Rhododendrons were bursting into blossom.

Ben could hardly keep his eyes on the road. Both he and Eva gaped at the magnificent forest. They came to another road that pushed into the heart of the big trees. At the end of this road they saw a beehive of human activity, a logging camp. Ben pulled over to the side of the road to make way for a team of oxen dragging out a large chunk of a redwood tree.

"Timberrrrr!" A shout echoed off in the forest. Ben heard a rush of wind and the crashing thud of a giant redwood hitting the ground. Next he heard dynamite blasts and the splintering of wood.

"They're cutting down trees that are thousands of years old," Eva said. "Shame on them! They don't know what they are doing. How are we ever going to replace these wonderful old treasures?"

"They are simply men making a living," Ben said.

"You're right, Ben. But they are also destroying

an environment that has taken thousands of years to evolve. My father thinks this may be the only forest like this left in the world."

"What of the jobs that these lumber mills offer? Why, hundreds, thousands, of people benefit from these logging practices. The logs are used to manufacture thousands of different items putting even more people to work. These people have families to support. There are more than enough trees to last hundreds of years."

"What will happen then?" Eva said.

There seemed to be no common ground between the two debaters. But both enjoyed the arguments because they could learn opposing viewpoints without the other person getting upset. To Ben and Eva it was merely a debate, and when finished they could discuss other issues that were of common interest.

Ben paused and looked over at Eva smiling. He was developing a fondness for this woman. "You know what I like about our discussions?" Ben said.

"I know," Eva said. "You're one of the few people who hasn't condemned me for my point of view. I appreciate that very much. Your input is valuable to me." They exchanged warm glances.

Ben turned the car around and soon they were back out on the highway again.

"Let's stop over there along the side of the road," Eva said. "I want to take a few pictures."

Ben pulled over and stopped. "Before taking any pictures let's follow that deer trail that goes into the forest."

"Okay," Eva said.

Ben lost track of time as they passed between the redwood Goliaths. It was a dark trail cushioned with decaying bark, wood, moss, and needles. The sun was hardly visible but Ben knew it was there because shafts of light sprayed through the trees. Huge green ferns radiated from the edge of the trail that tunneled ever deeper into the pristine forest.

"Oh, what's that?" Eva said as she jumped. A big antlered Roosevelt elk popped out of the underbrush and followed the trail ahead of them before leaping off through the trees. As the mist cleared, Ben heard birds sing merrily in the branches and saw Eva cock her head listening to a woodpecker as it hammered away on a snag. A huge tree lay prone, stretching away from the trail, almost out of sight. Its decaying bark and wood provided mulch for new trees to grow. Eva's hand sought out Ben's and they stumbled along as if they were the first to enjoy this exquisite path.

"We better get back," Ben finally said. Eva agreed. When they got back to the car Eva instructed Ben on how to set up her camera and tripod.

"Now I want you to go over there next to that large redwood. I want to show just how big the base of that tree is, to give my father a perspective." While Eva prepared to take the photograph, Ben couldn't help looking up at the monstrous trees. He felt small. Eva had her back to the road and Ben was getting antsy because it was taking Eva so long to adjust her camera.

"How much longer?" Ben asked.

"It takes a while to set up, please just relax."

As Ben stood there he saw a car approach. It was Tom! Ben could see a raised clenched fist and a snarling face as Tom passed by. Ben was dumbfounded and frightened. How did he get himself into this mess? No wonder Eva was terrified. Ben wanted to tell Eva what he had just seen but quickly chose to withhold what had happened. Eva had been concentrating so hard on taking her picture, she hadn't heard Tom's car. Eva took the picture.

"Perfect," she said. "Now, move over to the rhododendron, near the blossoms. And don't look so glum. Smile!" Ben did as he was instructed and forced out a smile.

After Eva was satisfied with her photographs they loaded her gear back in the car. Then they drove back to the highway. It was about three p.m. when they rolled into the oceanside town of Crescent City. They ate lunch in a small café. After their meal they climbed back into Ben's car and began their journey north, on the Roosevelt Highway, that would take them all the way to Astoria.

"Let's plan on staying at Brookings," Ben said. "It's the next large town, just over the Oregon border. We'll need our rest because I've heard the road north of there is treacherous."

"It could be even worse," Eva said, pointing to the darkness easing above the western horizon. "If it rains those roads will be impassable, won't they?"

"We're about to find out," Ben said.

When they crossed over the California line into Oregon the clouds were a little higher in the sky. They went through the small town of Harbor and then crossed over the new Chetco River Bridge.

"What a grand bridge!" Eva exclaimed. Gleaming steel arches sprang across the river in three beautiful arcs supported by concrete piers.

While crossing the magnificent structure, Ben looked up through the web of intertwining steel beams and marveled. Once across Ben said, "I've got to have pictures of this bridge to go with my article." So he stopped the car on the north side and they got out Eva's camera equipment.

"Back the car up so that it looks like it's just

coming off the bridge," Eva suggested. Ben carefully backed up, and Eva raised her hand indicating that was far enough. She placed her camera on the tripod and began framing the shot. She noticed through the viewfinder a car at the south approach to the bridge. She immediately tensed up. She saw the car stop, slowly turn around and drive away out of sight. Oh my, she thought to herself, he's still following us.

"Hurry up Eva, take the picture," Ben said.

Eva nervously focused her attention back on Ben and took the picture. She moved the tripod to a different location and took another and then another. Soon they were back in the car and once again driving north.

It wasn't long before they were driving on the main street of Brookings.

"Look at the azalea bushes," Eva said. They were interspersed between buildings, logging equipment and train cars. Eva and Ben stopped to get gas at the only station in town.

"How come there's not much lumber activity going on?" Ben asked the attendant.

"The logging mill closed down a year ago and hasn't reopened. The closing put most of the town's people out of work. We're just beginning to pull out of the slump thanks to the tourist trade, but this winter promises to be tough."

"Where can we spend the night?" Ben inquired.

"The Chetco Inn," replied the attendant, as he replaced the gas nozzle. "They have furnished rooms. Their owners are excellent cooks."

"Thanks," Ben said, paying the attendant. Then he drove the car back out onto the main street.

"I've read that there are more azaleas just north of here," Eva said. "They're supposed to be spectacular. Let's drive past town a ways and see if we can find them," Ben nodded in agreement.

Like a lantern, the sun hung in the western sky, touching the dark clouds. They came to a Y in the road. To the right a crude sign had an arrow pointing north and the words: *Gold Beach forty miles.* To the left was a new two-lane graveled road that led west to the ocean.

"This must be a finished segment of the Roosevelt Highway," Ben said. "Let's see where it ends." Ben drove until they came to a big piece of road machinery that blocked further travel. They got out and walked to the other side of the steam shovel. This was where the road ended. Thick brush, big rocks, short trees and ravines extended to the north.

"Oh, Ben," Eva said. "Look at the ocean. I've never seen it so blue. And those azalea blossoms are spectacular!" Extending west and covering the terrain almost to the oceans edge were acres and acres of azalea bushes. Red, and pink blossoms set the landscape ablaze with color. Ben noticed the sun's brightness fade as it slowly sank behind the dark clouds. The light's fading intensity made the colors even more vibrant.

"I must get photographs of this scene," Eva said. They removed the camera gear from the car and Ben set up Eva's tripod. "Darn!" She said, "I need color film. Why hasn't someone invented it?" Ben took out his notebook and noted the blossom colors. He desperately sought the words to retell what they were witnessing. They stood just inches apart as they beheld the beauty that lay before them.

To Eva, Ben was becoming more then just a friend. She appreciated the fact that he respected her as a woman, that he honored her opinion, that he was caring and thoughtful.

Eva turned to look at Ben. "I've longed to see this

sight for so long. It's absolutely wonderful."

Then she kissed Ben on the lips.

When their lips parted Ben's face reddened and he beamed. He was speechless. Oh, how I love this woman, he thought.

Darkness was creeping up on them. Ben came back to his senses.

"We have to get back to Brookings."

"Just one more picture," Eva said. Ben was in a state of euphoria as they folded the tripod and stashed it and the camera back in the car. But dark clouds were approaching fast.

Chapter Eight

That morning after Ben and Eva had left. Tom returned to the hotel. While talking to the clerk he noticed Ben Cooper's name on the registry.

"I'm trying to catch up with Mr. Cooper. I have some important information for him," Tom told the clerk.

"Wow," said the clerk. "This is exciting. Are you a reporter for the *Oregonian*, too?"

"Yeah, do you know which way they went?" Tom asked.

"Only that they're headed for the redwoods."

"Where's your phone?" Tom asked.

"Over by the rest rooms." The clerk pointed.

Now that I know where Ben works, Tom thought, maybe I can get some more information about where he's going.

Tom asked the operator for the phone number of the *Oregonian*. Once he had it he asked to be connected with the paper. "Hello, I'm trying to locate Ben Cooper. Do you know where I can find him?"

"He's on an assignment writing a story about the Roosevelt Highway. Would you like to leave a message?"

"No thank you. Good bye." Tom hung up. Ah-ha, he thought. They must be going to Crescent City and from there up the Oregon Coast to Astoria. Later that day he passed them taking pictures in the redwoods, then almost surprised them on the Chetco River Bridge.

From a windy knoll, Tom spotted them again south

of Brookings. He sat in his car watching them through his telescope. The window was rolled down and he could feel the brisk wind on his face. As the wind buffeted the car he had trouble keeping his telescope steady. On the passenger seat next to him lay his revolver, and next to that was a bottle of morphine. He had stolen the morphine from the veterinary lab at Oregon Agricultural College. He felt he would need these items if he ever hoped to get Eva back.

Tom had to put his telescope down, it was just too windy. With his unaided eye he could still see them but not as clearly. They stood as two dark spots facing the ocean in a sea of flowers. All of a sudden he saw the spots merge.

"You cheat!" He hissed, and his adrenaline began to flow like a raging river. His teeth clenched. He nervously ran his hand through his hair. Now I know what really happened, why you left me, he thought.

Tom didn't like being deceived. Eva had told him she would marry him! By God, she was going to marry him, too. He just needed to talk to her one more time. He knew he could convince her to keep her promise. He couldn't really understand why she had decided not to see him again. Hadn't he sent her flowers? Hadn't he apologized numerous times? Hadn't he made every effort to correct her misunderstanding about what really happened that night?

This was not what Tom had been taught at home. His father had told him that a woman was a man's property. The man should lead and woman was to follow. His mother had followed her husband, suppressing her own feelings and thoughts. This is the way a relationship was supposed to be. A man is entitled to go crazy when his woman is unfaithful, isn't he? Tom thought. He pulled out his flask and took a few gulps.

He picked up the revolver and checked it to make sure it was loaded. Then he laid it back on the seat.

I can hardly wait to jam this gun into Ben's stomach, he thought. I'm going to laugh as the bullet rips through his guts. The wind eased up enough for Tom to put the telescope back to his eye. He watched as they talked and laughed. He could see enough to tell that Eva was happy, really happy. He nervously pulled out a cigarette and tried to light it with a shaking hand. She'll pay, he thought. Then he noticed them driving back towards Brookings.

He didn't know how long it would take to get Eva back, but he knew eventually Ben and Eva would be careless. When that happened he would make his move. Overhead the sky was quickly filling with dark clouds and Tom could see a big rainstorm approaching. Night was advancing fast. The wind shook Tom's car. He took another swig from his flask and then returned it to his pocket. He drove slowly back to Brookings.

Chapter Nine

On Wednesday morning Ben and Eva were in the Chetco Inn's dining room about to eat breakfast. It was a huge room with a high ceiling and gaudy chandeliers. Heavy dark purple draperies surrounded the windows. Bright sunlight cast an irregular, wavering trapezoid on the oak floor. The tables were all festively decorated with colorful red-and white-tablecloths. Sitting on the tables was fresh fruit in blue-and-white bowls and preserves in glass jars. The tables also displayed colorful vases filled with freshly picked azaleas. Rich aromas of bacon, eggs, and pancakes piqued Ben's appetite.

Smoke from cigarettes drifted lazily in the air. Margaret Miller, the waitress, juggled plates of steaming food while walking to and from the kitchen. Most of the diners were loggers dressed in plaid shirts, their jeans held up by suspenders. They wore high-topped logging boots and a variety of brimmed hats. There were also a few well dressed business men reading the morning paper. Four workmen sat at a table next to Ben's. Margaret was very interested in the two journalists and hurried to their table with their order.

"I hope you'll write about my inn in your paper, Mr. Cooper. We always look forward to having people from Portland here." She placed the steaming food in front of them.

"I certainly will," Ben said. "Say, maybe you can help us with information on the roads around here.

What's the road like between here and Gold Beach?"

"From here to Pistol River it's a one lane stagecoach road. But, even stagecoaches have trouble making the run. That stretch has huge tree roots, fallen trees, rocks, and deep water holes. It's been improved slightly by motorists who have driven it. Because of the rain last night the road will be very muddy. It will require a lot of pick and shovel work."

"How many miles is it to Pistol River?" Ben asked.

"With all the curves, it's about twenty miles. But today after the rains, it's going to seem like sixty," Margaret replied. "If you make it through to Pistol River, the road from there to Gold Beach is very good. I'd advise you to wait a day before you drive to Pistol River. Give it time to dry up. However, the weather does look good for today."

"They'll be okay, Mrs. Miller," said a workman from the nearby table. "We're taking our horse team over that road to work on the new Roosevelt Highway. If they get stuck we can pull them out."

"That's very reassuring, Ben said. We're on a deadline and need to go today. What type of road work will your horses do there?"

"We'll be grading and clearing in preparation for putting down gravel. I wish you two the best of luck." He put down his coffee cup and turned his attention back to his group.

Ben and Eva finished their meal, paid Margaret, and went outside. They squinted in the bright morning light. They had packed the car earlier so they climbed into the coupe and drove off in a northeast direction. Soon they were the only car on the road. When they came to the Y in the road they turned east and headed up the hill. At first it wasn't steep, so they were able to move along. However, the tires slipped often.

"I better put on the tire chains," Ben said.

"I'll help," Eva said.

After an hour of work they were able to stretch the chains tightly over the back tires. Once again they were on their way. The chains helped, but Ben could feel the rear tires spinning often. Thick vegetation grew on both sides of the narrow road. The route was barely wide enough for one car. Ben knew the sun was shinning but the thick canopy overhead shrouded out much of the light. They slowly eased across small wooden bridges built over gushing mountain streams. Every once in a while they would come to an area where a farmer had cleared land for a homestead.

Just past one of these clearings they came to a big rock that had fallen from the hillside and lay in the center of the road. Ben recognized at once that they wouldn't be able to move it. So he decided that he and Eva would have to clear a path around it. After about three hours of strenuous labor—Eva hacking away with the hatchet and Ben shoveling—they were able to get the car past the obstruction. Once they were clear it wasn't long before Ben's coupe got stuck in soft mud at the base of a hill. Ben put some branches under the back tires and tried going up the hill again. He pushed the gas pedal to the floor. The tires spun wildly, moving the car just slightly up the hill. With the tires still spinning Ben lost control and the car slid back off the road into the forest, almost crashing into a tree. The soft spongy soil, swallowed the rear end of Ben's coupe, like wet cement.

"The director of my orphanage used to tell me how to get out of spots like this," Ben said.

"And how was that?" Eva asked.

"Dig ourselves out."

"I think we could dig for three days and never get

out of this mud," Eva said.

"While I'm digging around the tires you go cut some boughs off those cedars." Ben handed Eva the hatchet.

"Before cutting any boughs I'm taking pictures." Eva handed the hatchet back to Ben. Ben watched as she opened the door to get out. Her legs sank knee deep into the mud. She waded out of the car and fell.

"Ben!" She cried. "We're stuck in mud up to the running boards." She tried in vain to get up. Ben got out and sloshed to her rescue. He tried to help her up but the weight of Eva caused him to slip. He landed with a splash slopping more mud on Eva.

"Oh no, you've knocked my blue hat in the mud," Eva said. She struggled to get up, wresting herself from the sucking mud. Finally she was able to stand.

"Here's your hat," Ben said with a wry smile. He handed the soggy felt up to her.

"My hat's ruined!" She filled it with mud and dropped it on Ben. Mud dripped off Ben's face.

"Why did you do that? At least give me a hand up." Eva stood over Ben and tried to help him up, but lost her footing and landed on top of him. Mud and dirty water covered them both. Ben couldn't help smiling at their situation. He threw the waterlogged hat into the car. His smile turned to a chuckle and then a roar. Eva infected by the flood of laughter, began laughing too. Ben pushed Eva off of him and got up laughing so hard he had trouble keeping his balance. At that moment Eva pulled his leg out from under him and Ben fell like a hewed cedar crashing back to earth. That started another round of belly-aching laughter. Ben threw some mud at Eva. Eva reciprocated. They kept getting up, throwing mud, laughing, and falling back down.

Suddenly Ben heard the blast of a gunshot. A bullet punctured the inside of the opened car door.

"What the——?" Ben looked up, startled to sanity.

"Someone's shooting at us!" Eva cried. "Quick, get down behind the door." Both of them slid over to the protection of the opened door.

After a few minutes Ben peeked down the road.

"Get down," Eva warned.

"Its Tom I see him running away."

"Why is he running?"

"I don't know. Wait, Oh, I see why he ran. It's the men from breakfast and they're coming this way."

The leader, Sam Wilkes, was the first to arrive. "We heard a shot. Are you folks alright?"

"No," Ben said as he steadied himself holding onto the car door.

"A man with a limp ran past us just after the shot." Sam said. "He was headed back down the road. No way to catch him now. He's half way back to Brookings." Sam looked around at one of his men. "Bill, go back to town and report to Sheriff Jones. You can catch up with us later.

"Thanks," Ben said, still shaking.

There was a hesitation in Sam's voice as he turned back to Ben and Eva. Then he began laughing. "Look at you two! Been playing in the mud?"

Ben didn't find it so funny anymore. "Could your horses pull my car out of this mud?"

"We'll pull you out right away." Sam motioned with his hands for the workmen to get the horses in position. "John, you and Frank hook the chain up to the axle." The two men did as they were told. Then the horses slowly dragged the car out of the mud pit.

"How much farther is it to a good gravel road?" Ben asked.

"You've come over the worst of it. It's downhill after we get you to the top of that crest." Sam pointed to the hill.

"We can all walk to the top. Then we'll unhook the chain. You'll find the going a lot easier soon because the roads are drying out. It's only about five miles to good gravel. You should be able to make it to the Arizona Inn and a good bath before nightfall if all goes well."

It took a good two hours before the group reached the top of the hill.

"Thanks again," Ben said.

"Good luck," Sam said.

Eva waved to the men as she and Ben drove down the hill. Once out of sight Ben pulled the car over to the side of the road and they squished off their seats and out of the car. They covered the seats with towels. Then with the car between them they changed into dry cloths. Eva used one of the towels to vigorously dry off her hair. Dryer now, they climbed back into the car. With her hair still damp Eva put on her red felt brimless hat. Ben drove west towards the next completed section of the Roosevelt Highway.

Chapter Ten

Tom Bigalow sat in his car, raging at himself for bungling the abduction. He pounded his fist on the dash with frustration. How could he have missed? If it hadn't been for those men with the horses he would have had more time. He could've walked right up to Ben's car and shot Ben at point blank range. Ben was lucky this time. Once he had Ben out of the way it would be easy to get Eva. He'd be more careful next time and make sure there was no one following. He pounded his fist again, muttering, "You fool! You fool!"

He started the car. Backing up he noticed a small lane that went off the road. He backed into it, where the car was hidden by Oregon grape, vine maples, and huckleberry. He felt safe away from the main road. The road was too muddy for driving anyway and if he were to catch up with those horsemen they might not understand. For now, he would wait for the roads to dry out. Then he'd continue his pursuit.

He had just stepped out of the car to smoke a cigarette when he heard the sloshing of footsteps approaching from up the road. Through the bushes he could see it was one of the horsemen. Maybe he's headed back to Brookings to report the shooting, Tom thought. I've got to stop him. Tom casually walked out on the muddy road.

"Howdy," Tom said.

"Hi," Bill responded warily.

"Are those people alright?" Tom asked, inhaling

some smoke.

"They're frightened, but okay," Bill responded.

"What a stupid thing I did. I didn't even see them up there. I was shooting at a cougar that was running up the road. I was concentrating so hard on that damn cougar that I didn't notice the people. Afterwards I saw them and was scared silly, thinking I may have injured one of them. You're sure they're OK?"

"Yes, yes, they're fine."

"I was hoping to make a few extra bucks in bounty money by killing that cat. When I heard you fellows coming up the road I guess I panicked and ran. It was all a mistake. I'm really sorry I did that. You do understand, don't you?"

"Actually, I do." Bill said. "I almost killed my best friend not long ago when we were hunting deer. I had the buck in my sights when all of a sudden there was Adam between me and that buck. Fortunately I pulled up at the last instant. It was really close. I could've killed him. I'll go back and try and explain it to my boss. I'm sure he'll understand too. So long." And Bill headed back up the road.

Tom let out a sigh of relief and flicked his cigarette into the mud. He climbed back into his sedan and waited. If he comes back I'll have to kill him, Tom thought. Tom got comfortable on his front seat by stretching his legs across the passenger seat. Soon his eyelids closed and his chin fell to his chest. Tom drifted off to sleep.

Chapter Eleven

"I like your red hat better than the blue one," Ben said.

"Thank you," Eva said. "I'll remember that."

"Look, the new Roosevelt Highway. It'll be a lot easier driving once we reach it," Ben said. From his vantage point, driving down the hill, he saw the highway snaking northward, following the curvature of the coast line.

They finally came to the freshly graveled road. Ben took out his note pad and wrote about the work on the Roosevelt Highway south of Pistol River. He noted the horse-drawn graders and the steam-operated caterpillars that were clearing away the brush and leveling out a roadbed. He'd also seen two steam shovels removing piles of shrubbery and dirt.

"Glad we don't have to go that way," Ben said. "The highway to Gold Beach looks new." And off they sped at 30 miles an hour, creating a small dust storm.

Ben wanted a cigarette badly, especially after the frightening attack on them. Eva deserved someone braver to handle her problems with Tom. She needed someone who was courageous, not a weakling like him. In desperation he pulled out his flask and took a big gulp.

"Here, have a swig of this," Ben said. And he handed the flask to Eva. "It'll help steady your nerves after what we've been through."

"No thanks!" Eva said. She handed the flask back

to Ben. "I hope that the man Sam sent to Brookings alerts the authorities about Tom trying to kill us."

"Tom's a lunatic. Hopefully he'll be in custody soon."

"I'm really scared, Ben. Tom is no ordinary man. He's smart and manipulative. One of us almost got shot back there. He'll stop at nothing. I never thought he would go this far."

"Listen, are you sure you want to continue this journey with me? I'm not the best of protectors."

"I have an important assignment. I need to write about the way our forests are being devastated. I feel passionate about this Ben. I must continue. If not with you, then I would do it with someone else. Besides, if I went home I would be harassed there too. Ben, I know you don't have confidence in your abilities to handle danger, but I see something else in you, a strength and potential that can handle difficult situations. It must be hard for you, considering my views on the environment and Tom's stalking. I'm sorry for what's happening but I beg you to keep me with you."

"All right then, we're in this thing together all the way to Astoria."

After about ten miles of spectacular ocean views from cliffs and headlands, Ben slowed the coupe to 20 miles an hour on the edge of the small fishing and logging community of Gold Beach. It was a busy town that faced the Pacific Ocean. Makeshift logging trucks filled the street. Ben saw sailing vessels in the peaceful harbor. The main street ended at the Rogue River where an old rutted road turned abruptly east, skirting the river's edge.

"Look," Eva said. "There's a man in a boat, reeling in a fish."

"It's supposed to be the best salmon fishing in

Oregon," Ben responded.

Soon Ben was busy negotiating the rugged river road. He was grateful for the drier conditions but the road was still very rough, with big boulders, ruts, and sharp curves. After four miles they came to a small ferry landing. The sun was plunging towards the horizon. It had taken practically all day just to reach the Rogue River.

"Look, Ben," Eva said. "Here comes the ferry now."

"I hope that contraption will get us across the river," Ben frowned. They waited as the ferry man maneuvered the little craft to the landing dock. Once it was securely attached, a Buick sedan drove ashore. The car slowed as it came along side the coupe. The driver waved and drove on.

"That'll be fifty cents," Mr. Bagnell said. "I always collect payment before taking anyone across. Oh and here's a copy of the latest *Curry County Reporter*, the newspaper from Gold Beach."

Ben paid Mr. Bagnell and handed the paper to Eva. Ben was worried about the little ferry. It wobbled as he drove on board. There was just enough room for one car.

"Please stay in the car." Mr. Bagnell untied the rope, started the ferry's little diesel engine, and the boat slowly moved out into the current. Once in the middle of the river, Ben and Eva enjoyed the spectacular view. As they bounced and bobbed over the rushing water they saw seals poke their glistening noses through the water, making little ripples. Hundreds of birds flew overhead, mostly ducks. Gulls flew in the wake of the boat trying to snag the salmon parts thrown over the side by Mr. Bagnell.

Ben couldn't take his eyes off of Eva with her bright red hat. She was like a smiling giddy child fascinated with the wondrous sights. He sensed she was aware, for the first time in her life, that what she was observing confirmed what she had written: That this scenic area had to be preserved. Ben shook his head. She almost had him thinking like her.

As they approached the north bank the ferry careened and wobbled in the current, but the little craft held its course and they were able to reach the landing.

"The tide's coming in," Mr. Bagnell said. "I'll only be able to do one more trip across the river and then I'll be done for the day." A car waited on the north landing. It'd be Mr. Bagnells last fare, Ben thought.

Once on the stable roadbed, Ben was thankful that the rain had not returned. This part of the Roosevelt Highway was graded but not surfaced with gravel. He would have to make a note of this once they got to the Arizona Inn. The surrounding landscape was also catching Ben's attention.

He was astounded by the many wildflowers lining the road. Ben saw Eva put down her newspaper and gaze out in wonder. Spread out before them was a panorama of color unequalled by any oil painting Ben had ever seen.

"Irises, lupine, larkspur, Indian paintbrush, daisies, buttercups, and bright tiger lilies, wow!" Eva said.

Ben thought Eva more beautiful than any of these flowers, especially with her colorful red hat.

"I wonder how many more years we can be privileged to see this type of beauty?" Eva asked.

"What do you mean?"

"If I could just capture this beauty on color film maybe people would see it for what it is. Then maybe they'd call a halt to civilizing this part of the state."

"People aren't trying to destroy the landscape," Ben objected. "They just want to see it and to use it."

"Even this road is an encroachment. It will bring

the masses—in their new autos. They'll walk over everything, cut down everything and kill everything. Then someday in the future they'll try in vain to replace it."

Eva was quiet for a moment. Then she asked, "What's that big mountain looming up ahead?"

"Humbug Mountain," Ben replied. "You're exaggerating everything, Eva. Why this road is a blessing! It will save these little coastal towns. You're right about one thing, that this road will bring an explosion of commerce and traffic. But, the people of these coastal communities will be the beneficiaries."

"Humbug yourself!" Eva said. "I guess my father is right. The people with money are able to set the agenda. They're bent on destroying huge old trees and smothering exquisite fields of beauty, all the while saying it's for the public good. The workers don't see what the lumber barons are doing to the land. They are leading everyone in the wrong direction. It's as maddening as when I tried to explain to the sheriff that Tom tried to rape me. The sheriff just laughed in my face."

"Tom tried to rape you?" Ben asked surprised.

"Yes," Eva said quietly.

"That son-of-a-bitch!" Ben exclaimed.

As they drove down the narrow road, waves crested out on the Pacific Ocean.

Eva picked up the paper.

"Here's an advertisement in the paper for the Arizona Inn," she said. "They have family style meals. It's near the beach and out of the wind. That might be a nice place to stay."

I just hope Tom doesn't show up, Ben thought to himself.

Chapter Twelve

Tom awoke later in the day. He got out of his car to check the condition of the road and found it dry enough to drive on. He drove slowly out from his hiding place and onto Pistol River Road. Then he drove up the hill to the crest, the same crest that the horsemen had dragged Ben's car to. He noticed that it would be 'easy sailing' down the slope to the ocean and the Roosevelt Highway. I'm only a few hours behind them, he thought. I'll catch them this evening while they're asleep.

Once he was on the Roosevelt Highway the sun slipped below the horizon and darkness approached quickly. He sped north on cliffs and through dense forests. Once he glimpsed a black bear in his head lamps. He even saw a coyote run across his path. Then, suddenly, he saw a raccoon emerge from the roadside brush. He swerved to hit it, and his front tire rolled over the poor creature's head. Tom laughed jubilantly as his back tire finished off what the front had started. The sudden bump almost threw the car off the road, but he swerved back, smiling all the time. He knew he was making good time.

In Gold Beach he had to stop for gas. He just barely caught the attendant who was closing for the night.

"Fill it up," Tom said.

"Yes sir," the attendant replied.

"Did you see a coupe with a man and woman drive by recently?"

"Why, yes, I saw them go by about three hours ago."

"Thanks." Tom paid the attendant through his window, started the engine, and turned on his head lamps. He drove out onto the main street of town and headed north. It was dark now, but he still managed to locate the eastbound bumpy road that followed the Rogue River. It was slow going, and he almost went over the edge on one sharp curve. I wish I had more light, he thought. Still he kept on. "Ouch!" He winced after hitting a big bump that threw his head up against the roof. Sore and aching, he finally reached the ferry landing. But no one was there. Tom used his head lamps to light up the sign that was above the ferry landing.

Mr. Bagnell proprietor can be found two houses up on the right hand side of the road. There will be an additional fee of one dollar for night crossings.

Tom got out and walked up the road. At the second house he noticed the door was ajar. He pushed it open. "Anyone home?"

"I'm out back," Mr. Bagnell responded.

Tom walked around the house and found the elderly Mr. Bagnell seated on a stump eating a freshly cooked salmon. The fire jumped madly in the darkness as if trying to reach the leaves of the creek side alders. It lit up Mr. Bagnell's bearded face and his surrounding campsite. He was wearing a tilted, wide-brimmed hat. Tom saw Bagnell throw fish bones into the fire.

"I need to get across the river immediately," Tom said.

"Sorry, but I can't do that." Bagnell took a big bite of biscuit. "The tides up. I won't be crossing again until tomorrow morning."

Tom held out a fistful of money. "I have to get across tonight! I'll pay double or even triple."

"Son, simmer down! I don't want to lose my ferry

just to satisfy your whim. If I went across tonight, why, we'd end up in China. I don't want to do that. You can camp at the ferry landing and when the tide has ebbed, tomorrow morning, we'll make the crossing. That's earlier than I usually go. Have your money ready, it'll be two dollars and fifty cents more." With that he threw his food scraps into the fire, rose, and went into the house.

Tom stared at the fire in despair. Would he ever catch up with Eva?

Chapter Thirteen

Ben and Eva drove into the parking area in front of the Arizona Inn. It was an elegant two-story house with a gabled roof and three dormers. Ben and Eva entered through the windowed porch. The dining room inside was spotlessly clean. Young girls were everywhere, serving food to the loggers, road construction men, and tourists. Smells of fried chicken, fish, and fresh baked pies filled the room. The wood floors gleamed and the many windows provided plenty of light, even with the declining daylight. It was a busy place.

"Excuse me," said a girl carrying a tray of food on her way to a table.

Ben and Eva weaved their way past the tables and girls to a registration desk in the lobby. They registered as man and wife. After carrying their suitcases upstairs to their room they returned to the dining room. A waitress in a brightly colored floral dress escorted them to a square table next to a window. She gave them menus and lit a candle on their table.

"Mrs. Hall is frying salmon tonight and it includes mashed potatoes, gravy, vegetable, and biscuits."

Both Ben and Eva's eyes lit up. "We'll take two salmon dinners," Ben said. Ben and Eva relaxed in their chairs. Ben felt a cool breeze from the opened window.

"After dinner I'm going to rewrite my notes on the Roosevelt Highway," Ben said. "I want to include information on that rickety Rogue River ferry, and

I'm certainly going to include something about this wonderful inn."

"I'm going to rewrite my article on the redwoods," Eva said. "At the rate they're chopping down these old trees there won't be any forest left for future generations. Plus, I want to write about the acres and acres of azaleas around Brookings, and the masses of flowers we saw between here and the Rogue River."

Although the two talked about journalism, they avoided the topic that concerned them the most. Ben wished secretly that Tom would just go away and leave them alone.

The waitress brought two steaming dinners and a pot of fresh coffee. Their mouths watered with the sight of the tempting meal. When their coffee cups were filled the waitress moved off to a neighboring table. Ben picked up a golden biscuit and slathered butter and jelly on it. Eva did the same. Ben cut a juicy morsel from the baked salmon and speared it with his fork.

Suddenly two loud blasts pierced the evening's calm, followed by two more blasts. Ben and Eva dropped their biscuits. Ben turned the table on its side, spilling their food on the floor. They both huddled behind the table for protection.

A waitress rushed over to them. "What's wrong?"

"Get down!" Eva said. "Someone is shooting at us. Next to me, quick!"

"The girl laughed. I don't think so! "That's just the sound of a car backfiring as it comes down the steep hairpin curve."

Ben and Eva looked at each other in surprise and embarrassment. They quickly got up. Everyone in the room was staring at them.

"Please, let us help you clean up the mess," Eva said.

Ben quickly paid for their meal. They meekly

walked from the dinning room and went upstairs.

The next morning they drove from the inn up the steep incline that tunneled through the forest. They drove on a good gravel road. They came to the hairpin curve and crested a mountain ridge. Then it was downhill with more curves. The road had been gouged from the side of a steep cliff, suspended above the ocean. They could hear the crashing surf below.

"You're awfully close to the edge," Eva said, a little frightened.

"It shouldn't be as bad once we get through this mountainous region."

"I have to stop and rest a while. I'm getting car sick. Let's stop at that overlook. Please?" Eva pleaded.

Ben parked the coupe at the wide spot in the road where they could hear the waves crashing hundreds of feet below. Ben took out his notebook and wrote about the dense forests and curvy roads they had just passed. When he finished Eva was ready to move on. They drove down from the heights of Humbug Mountain and landed in the small town of Port Orford.

Port Orford bustled with logging activity.

"I need to get some photos of the logging trucks," Ben said. "I'm curious what type of lumber is being transported and to where."

Ben drove up a side road until he came to a small logging operation. He pulled over next to a truck. Three loggers were in the forest felling a large one-hundred-eighty-foot cedar tree. Two men were standing on opposite ends of a springboard that was inserted in the tree four feet off the ground. They worked feverishly chopping out a big groove. Their logging boots danced as they chopped in a rhythmic cadence. Flakes of wood scattered around the base of the big tree. They wore long sleeved thermal tops and had suspenders holding up their denim pants. Sweat darkened their chests. A huge two-man saw rested against the trunk.

Some of the trees in the forest were spindly—like skinny, starving people. Other trees dwarfed everything else—the big Douglas firs, spruce, red cedars, and a few Port Orford white cedars. Some of the branches on the trees were draped with green moss. Scattered on the ground were fern, maple shoots, and dead logs in various stages of decay.

"Ben, I need your help setting up my camera and tripod," Eva said. "I want to take a picture of those men chopping down that tree."

A burly logger came over to where they were working setting up Eva's equipment. "What's going on?"

"We're from the *Oregonian* newspaper," Ben replied. "We're doing a story on the Roosevelt Highway. I wonder if I could ask you a few questions."

"OK, but I don't have a lot of time."

"What type of tree are your men chopping down?" Ben asked.

"That's a Port Orford white cedar," the logger said proudly. "I specialize in cutting them."

"How can you tell a Port Orford cedar from all the rest?"

"They're conical," Eva piped in.

"They look like Christmas trees," the logger said. "And the wood is in big demand over in Japan. They use them for telephone poles and specialty items. Plus we use them locally too."

"How do you get these trees to market?" Ben asked.

"I'm paid by the foot at the big Marshfield lumber mills. You might say I'm an expert in Port Orford cedar. They only represent about ten percent of all the trees in the forest, so it takes experienced people like me to find them and bring them to market. I'm paid big money for what I find. Why go to the gold mines when the gold is right here in these trees?"

"Do you mind if we take pictures of your operation here?"

"Not at all," the logger said. "But I'd better get back to help my men. I have to pound a wedge in that tree they're working on. Be careful now."

The loggers chopping the tree could see that Eva wanted to take their picture so they stopped for a minute and posed looking directly into Eva's camera. Next Eva took a picture of the log truck. Ben wrote while she did her work. They finished about the same time. Then they loaded the camera gear into the car and drove back to the Roosevelt Highway.

"What's happening here is exactly what my father has warned against in his writings," Eva said. "They're cutting just one species of tree—in this case the Port Orford white cedar. Each type of evergreen is essential to a healthy forest. My father says the whole forest will be lost if this type of destruction is allowed to continue."

"It's a living for these people, and a hard living at that," Ben said. "I admire their tenacity and endurance."

"It makes me sick to see these huge old trees cut down. Once down, their real purpose in life is destroyed."

"Maybe their purpose in life is the homes and ships they are used for."

"Their purpose is to propagate life," Eva said.

About eight miles north of Port Orford they came to a sign with an arrow pointing west that read *12 miles to Cape Blanco*.

"We've got to stop at Cape Blanco and see the

lighthouse," Eva said.

Ben drove west on the dirt road.

"There it is on the edge of that headland," Eva said. "I have to get a picture."

Ben assisted Eva with her tripod and camera gear, setting it up so she could take a picture. The wind jolted the tripod about. Ben hoped Eva could get a clear photograph. Off in the distance they heard gun shots and sea lion barks. Seagulls circled overhead.

"I need to get closer to the lighthouse," She said. Despite a powerful wind, Eva managed to take a few more pictures. Ben watched as she walked to the edge of the cliff and looked seaward. He walked up behind her. The reef below was covered with sea lions and birds of all kinds.

"Ben, how could they!" Eva said, very disturbed. "Those men down there are clubbing, stabbing, and shooting those helpless sea lions. We have to stop them!"

"Eva, please! Let's get out of here. Those men are hunting. If we interfere they're liable to shoot us."

"I don't call that hunting," She said. "I call that mutilation."

"Wait, Eva!" Ben said.

Eva's red hat flew off her head as she started climbing down the cliff. Ben caught it in mid air and stuffed the hat in his back pocket. He climbed down after her.

Ben saw her dress flutter out in all directions. The wind blew stiffly, as if demonic forces were trying to keep her from helping the sea lions. Down she went, from rock to rock and foothold to foothold with Ben right behind her.

"Stop, Eva! Please, stop!"

Tears blew off her face. Her lips were lines of

determination and showed a fierce tension that Ben had never seen her display before. She reached the bottom and was about to step onto the reef screaming all the while.

"Stop killing those sea lions, you bullies!"

But her voice was lost in the gale force winds and waves. Just as she made one step onto the reef, Ben grabbed her from behind. With surprising strength he lifted her off the rocks and threw her over his right shoulder like a bag of potatoes.

Eva was crying. "Put me down! I have to stop them. Can't you see what they're doing?" She kicked and banged her fists on Ben's back. Ben held her firmly and slowly maneuvered back up a less precarious route. Once back on top Ben gently put her down. The wind continued to blow, dampening the sounds of the hunters from the reef. Eva fell to the ground weeping. Ben thought she would never stop. Her body heaved up and down and her sobs were soft mournful cries that only Ben could hear. Slowly she regained her composure and sat up.

"You're right, Ben," She said softly. "This time you're right. I was going to shame those brutes into quitting. But it wouldn't have worked. Those people are under a spell. Only when the seals are gone forever will they wake up and think, 'What have we done?' Of course by then it will be too late."

"I know how you feel."

Eva wiped her cheeks and stood up. Ben gave Eva her red hat and she adjusted it back on her head. "Thank you."

Sadly, they walked back to Ben's car. Carefully they picked up the tripod and camera and stowed it. Ben backed the coupe up, turned around, and drove towards the Roosevelt Highway. Once on the highway they continued north to Bandon.

For a few agonizing minutes, their minds had been taken off of Tom Bigalow.

Chapter Fourteen

Tom could hardly sleep that Wednesday night.
He had trouble finding a comfortable position in the
backseat of his car. He felt tired and sore when the light
of morning woke him. His beard and mustache were
growing and his body smelled. He hadn't bathed or
shaved in over two weeks. Fog shrouded the outside
world. "Oh no," he mumbled and then thought:
another delay.

"Damn it! At this rate I'll never catch them." He
opened the back door and got out of the car. He stood
and stretched. Then he ran his hand through his hair
and yawned. I've got to get across this confounded
river, he thought. He could hear the river but couldn't
even see it. His pulse was racing as he sat on the
running board and stared into the fog. And then, the
fog began to lift. There before him lay a scene of idyllic
beauty. It's about time, he thought.

The deep blue Rogue River rushed to the sea, amid
the green forest. Overhead a blue sky was dappled
with white wispy clouds. The fresh salt air tingled
in his nostrils. Tom opened the car door and climbed
in. He drove closer to the dock where the ferryboat
bobbed and thudded against pilings.

"Good morning." Mr. Bagnell greeted Tom as he
walked up to his car window. "It's a glorious Thursday.
Still, I'd like payment before I take you across."

"Let's get on with it." Tom paid the man.

Once Tom was across the river he looked back and

saw old Bagnell staring at him. "What are you starring at, you old fool?" Tom shifted into first gear, spraying gravel. His tires finally grabbed hold and the car sped out onto the road.

He drove as fast as possible, trying to make up for lost time. There was once again meaning to Tom Bigalow's existence: his desire to kidnap Eva and make her his possession. Surely, a man of his brilliance could complete this simple task. In this reckless state of mind he drove past the Arizona Inn and barely made it around the famous hairpin curve. One thing Tom instinctively knew was that while they played around kissing and writing he would be catching up to them.

Chapter Fifteen

It was about one p.m. when Ben and Eva drove into the small logging and fishing community of Bandon.

"I'm hungry," Eva said. "Let's get a loaf of bread at that bakery."

"Okay," Ben said. He stopped in front of a little store with a sign over the door, *BAKERY*. Eva went in and bought a loaf of fresh white bread. When she returned Ben could smell the tantalizing aroma rising from the sack. They drove to the banks of the Coquille River, where they noticed a salmon cannery.

"Are you thinking what I'm thinking," Ben said.

"Yes," Eva replied. "Let's get a can of salmon and have a picnic on the riverbank."

"That sounds good to me," Ben said.

After their picnic stop, they went back to the Roosevelt Highway driving east along the river towards the town of Coquille. Ben made a mental note of the good gravel they'd been driving on all the way from Humbug Mountain. At the rate they were traveling, they'd easily be in Marshfield by three p.m. From the town of Coquille they drove towards Marshfield over a concrete road—one of the smoothest they had been on since Corvallis. They smiled as they sailed along with nary a bump. Halfway to Marshfield they came to a sign pointing to the Coos Bay's golf club. Ben turned into the parking lot.

"Why are we stopping here," Eva said.

"Jess insisted that I include information on all the

golf courses on the Coast."

Tom Stack, the course professional, came out of the club house to greet them.

"Welcome to our course," he said. "Will you be playing today?"

"Not today," Ben replied. "We're journalists with the *Oregonian*. My editor expressly wanted me to find out about this new course."

"As you can see, we have a wonderful country setting for our nine-hole course."

"When did you open?" Ben asked.

"Please come inside to my office and I'll give you all the information you need." Once seated inside Mr. Stack's office he rattled on and on about the merits of his golf course. "The Coos Country Club was organized in 1923. The par for the new course is thirty-four. It's five thousand seven hundred yards long and cost thirty thousand dollars to build."

Ben studiously took notes. Mr. Stack finished the interview by saying, "Of course, we'd appreciate any advertising you could give us in the *Oregonian*."

"I'm sure my editor will do what he can. Could I use your phone? I need to call the *Coos Bay Times* editor and ask him some questions."

"Sure." He pushed his desk phone over to Ben. "Just dial operator and tell her where you want to call." Ben did what he'd been instructed to do. Soon he heard a voice at the other end of the line.

"This is the *Coos Bay Times*. May I help you?"

"This is Ben Cooper from the Portland *Oregonian* I'd like to talk with your editor." After a short pause, Ben heard a man's voice. "Hello, I'm Sam Thomas, editor of the *Times,* what can I do for you?"

"I need to get some information about the Roosevelt Highway, if you have time."

"I'll make time. I can assure you, I have lots of information about the highway. Can you drop by in an hour? I'll meet you at the front door to the newspaper office."

Ben hung up the phone, thanked the golf pro for his help, and headed for the car. Eva ran to keep up. Ben could hardly wait to drive on the concrete road again. They rolled over the smooth texture all the way to Marshfield right up to the front door of the *Coos Bay Times*. Sam Thomas met the couple at the front door as promised. He ushered them into his office, a room much like Jess's office. He closed the door and offered them seats. Sam sat behind his huge oak desk and looked at Ben and Eva as if he were on a throne.

Sam was a small man, immaculately dressed with suit and tie. He had a neatly trimmed mustache under his pointed nose. His black hair was parted in the middle and glittered with gel.

"I didn't know you had a companion," Sam said.

"I'd like you to meet Eva Barton," Ben said.

"Pleased, I'm sure," Sam said, eying Eva suspiciously. "Now what can I do for you two?"

"The Roosevelt Highway has affected your town in many ways. Would you care to say how?"

"Since you drove here from the south you no doubt saw that the road still needs a lot of work. But once it's completed I believe it will affect our economic prosperity in a number of ways. First, it provides a road for shipping our manufactured products to California. The uncertainty of shipping everything by the sea will no longer be an obstacle. Second, the highway connects us to other coastal communities. Third, and probably the most important, the highway brings in tourist dollars. People from California and other places are coming in droves, driving their new autos, camping, fishing and hunting. Many come just to see the coastal scenery. The highway has also made logging easier. More logs are now being cut than at any time in the past. But maybe I shouldn't talk so much about our local logging achievements with this young woman in the room." He narrowed his eyes at Eva.

"What do you mean?" Eva asked.

"Aren't you the Eva Barton who writes those inflammatory articles accusing the logging industry of decimating our coastal forests?" Sam stared at Eva.

"Yes," Eva said. "But I can hardly call them inflammatory when all I write is the truth."

"And your father, isn't he that radical college professor?" Sam asked.

"He's not a radical. What we have tried to point out is that the logging industry should be brought under control so that we can save some of our old forests. Do the logging companies plan on cutting down every single tree?"

"My dear, the logging industry employs more workers then any other industry on the Oregon Coast. Why, we have enough trees in our forests to last thousands of years. While you're driving up the Coast, be sure to notice how many people are employed by working in our forests. Maybe you can report that to your father. This year alone our logging production has exceeded four hundred and fifty million feet of lumber. And, Miss Barton, we haven't run out of trees yet. Really now, shouldn't you refrain from making such wild accusations?"

"Sir, you're not only destroying trees that are hundreds of years old, but the forest habitat as well. South of here they are destroying the redwood forests that are thousands of years old. How can you replant a forest that is a thousand years old? How many other plants, trees, and animals will be made extinct by this annihilation?"

"My dear, you're overdramatizing. Millions of dollars are being poured into our communities because of lumber. Schools, police, fire protection, and new roads are all financed with money from the logging industry. Even the construction of the Roosevelt Highway is being financially helped by the logging industry. The owners of our logging companies are generous men." Sam's face was getting red.

"I'm not overdramatizing anything," Eva snapped back. "When whole mountainsides are stripped of their trees, our pristine forests are devastated. My father says there's more to a forest than trees."

"Calm down, my dear. I can see you are very disturbed by this topic. Let's get back to Ben's original question about the highway." He looked at Ben. "The highway is not only affecting industry and tourism but is helping towns like ours develop our infrastructure to accommodate the influx of more people."

Ben studiously took notes as Sam spoke of facts and figures showing the increase of the town's prosperity due to the building of the highway.

"It's imperative that we finish this highway and the sooner the better," Sam stated. "It's been a long hard fight getting our share of the state and federal funds to help with construction. What's wrong with those idiots in the state highway commission's office anyway? Why don't they recognize the treasure we have here on the Coast? I'm at loss to understand. They dole out money to finish other state highway projects, yet they leave us on the Coast empty handed. Put that in your newspaper! Why, if it wasn't for the logging industry revenue, our road system would be deplorable."

"There are other ways to create revenue than

chopping down our forests," Eva said.

"Name one!" Sam roared.

"Tourism," Eva said. "Tourists don't want to see clearcuts. If we were to save the forests we could make our state a destination for tourists from all over the world. It would be an industry that would last for generations, an industry our grandchildren would be proud of. If the logging companies continue on their current path of destruction, then our grandchildren won't have anything."

"Preposterous!" Sam stood up. "What do you think about this, Ben?"

"I feel the same way you do. Still, I've come to appreciate Eva's view. She's pretty determined in her efforts to save our coastal forest."

"Rubbish. I say rubbish to the both of you. Control logging companies? Save our forests? I've heard enough of this outlandish talk, both of you leave my office at once."

Ben and Eva got up to leave. But, then Ben turned and faced Sam. "Have you had any information come across your desk concerning a man named Tom Bigalow?"

"No, I haven't." Sam snapped. "Why?"

"He tried to kill us a couple of days ago. We were hoping the authorities had been alerted. He's been stalking and harassing Eva." Ben put his hand on the doorknob.

"I haven't heard a word about it," Sam said. "Now get out."

Lying on Sam's desk was an article from the Corvallis *Times Gazette*:

KILLER AT LARGE

The bodies of Mr. and Mrs. Bigalow were discovered in their home by a friend Monday evening. Mr. Bigalow

had been shot in the chest and Mrs. Bigalow had been
strangled. Authorities believe they were killed by their
son Tom. Anyone with information as to where Tom
can be found, is requested to contact the Corvallis
police Department.

Sam picked up his phone and dialed a number.

"Is that you, Bert?" Sam asked.

"Yes. What's up Sam?"

"Eva Barton and her journalist friend just left my office. It seems a young man by the name of Tom Bigalow is trying to kill them. He's already killed his own parents. The Corvallis police want information on Tom. They want me to publish a story so they can get the public's help locating him. You know, of course, that Miss Barton is the one who's been bad-mouthing you about your logging techniques. What do you think we should do?

"Wait for a week. Then publish the story about Bigalow," Bert said. "This may be a legal way to get rid of a very big thorn in my side."

As Ben and Eva walked out of the newspaper office darkness was creeping over Marshfield.

Blakely Kidnapped

Chapter Sixteen

It was late in the afternoon on Thursday when Tom drove up to the Bandon fish cannery where Ben and Eva had purchased fish. The clerk told Tom that they had come through about three hours before.

"Is there a short cut to Coos Bay?" Tom asked.

"Yes," the clerk said. "Take the Seven Devils Road. It's dried considerably and you should make good time. The only hitch is that you'll have to cross the Coquille River on the old ferry. That ferryboat is a relic, but it works. It floats from the south bank to the north with the current. Then the old man who runs the ferry, Mr. Simmons, pulls it back with a cable attached to a diesel operated winch. Turn left when you come to the Coquille River. You can't miss it."

It was seven thirty p.m. when Tom pulled up onto the bumpy ferry landing. Mr. Simmons came out of a small shack to greet him. He was a heavyset man, dressed in dirty coveralls.

"That'll be thirty cents," Mr. Simmons said in an unusually loud voice.

"I'm in a hurry and need to get across as soon as possible," Tom said while paying the man.

"What did you say?" Mr. Simmons responded, a hand cupped to his ear.

"I need to get across the damned river!"

"You don't have to get mad. I'll get you there." Tom Simmons started up his diesel motor. The wire cable grew taut and jerked the small raft from the other side of the river. As the cable slowly wrapped around the large steel spool, the raft edged across the river. Halfway across, the diesel motor sputtered to a stop.

Tom got out of his car and shouted, "What's wrong?"

"Must need gas," Simmons shouted back. He filled up the motor's gas tank and tried to start it. The motor wouldn't start. Tom, was getting frustrated, and walked over to where Simmons stood. Tom ran his hand through his hair.

"Fix the damned thing!"

"I know what it is," Simmons said. He fiddled with a valve but that didn't work. Scratching his head he said, "Maybe it's the carburetor." So he set about adjusting that finicky device. "Stand back, I'm trying her again." He pulled the rope with all his might. Nothing happened.

Tom got back into his car. He thought about driving the highway through the town of Coquille, but he was so tired his eyelids grew heavy.

Two hours later, Tom was awakened by a rap on his car window.

"I got it fixed," Simmons said.

"What time is it?" Tom said.

"It's nine thirty," Simmons replied.

"Why, you fat fool, it's taken you all this time to fix that motor?"

"Don't get me riled or you won't get across at all," Simmons said. "Now let's load your car. Once you've crossed the river make sure you untie the raft so I can reel it back."

Tom drove his vehicle on the bobbing raft. Once across, Tom purposely left the raft tied to the dock. As he drove away he noticed Mr. Simmons getting into a rowboat. That'll show that old fool, Tom thought.

Looking ahead he saw thick fog moving in. It seemed to take forever inching along on the barely discernible road, before he finally arrived at Coos Bay. He could hear water rippling on the shore when he brought his car to a stop. It was well past midnight and Tom was tired. So he prepared for another night's sleep on the back seat of his car.

Blakely

Kidnapped

Chapter Seventeen

Ben and Eva left the Marshfield hotel about seven a.m. on Friday. They had to cross Coos Bay on the *Roosevelt*. The ferry was approaching the landing where they waited. Their vehicle was first in line. Behind them cars were starting to line up. There was even a horsedrawn wagon.

"We're in luck," said the man next in line. "We'll be able to get aboard. Usually it takes hours to get on the ferry. They only take eight cars. This early in the morning is the best time to cross."

"How long will it take to get across?" Ben inquired.

"It'll take about forty five minutes to reach Glasgow." The man replied. "That's the landing on the other side of the bay."

Ben heard a steam whistle and saw a puff of white smoke shoot up in the air from the approaching ferry. The steam stack rose five feet above the captain's raised steering compartment. Prominently displayed on the compartment was the ferry's name, *ROOSEVELT*. Underneath the captain's quarters was a waiting room for the passengers. Encircling the raised midship were parked cars. The steam engine propelled the craft between the tall pilings that led up to the landing. Deck hands lowered a connecting ramp. Ben listened to the cars' motors start up. He felt the breeze as the cars drove past him to the mainland.

"We can take vehicles now," shouted Captain Graham. He was all dressed up in his tidy blue uniform, with a tilted naval cap. Ben was the first to drive onto the ferryboat. He carefully drove to the far end.

"Not too far," Eva cautioned. "You'll drive us into the bay."

"We're okay," Ben said. "We'll be the first off."

"I hope that doesn't mean first into the bay," Eva jested.

The other vehicles took their places. A four-foot fence lined the sides of the craft. Again the steam engine spewed a white cloud and the whistle tooted. They were off and moving toward the other side of the bay.

"I hope I don't get seasick," Eva said.

"We won't be on it long enough for that," Ben said. "Let's get out of the car and watch the sights." Ben and Eva stood at the ferry's fence under a lifeboat that hung above them. They held their arms around each others' waists. The wind whipped at their clothing and faces. They watched the big and small fishing vessels, some going out to sea and some returning. They saw big ocean going steamers, and sloops loaded with lumber. They watched the wildlife, gulls soaring overhead and cormorants with their wings outstretched perched on buoys. Off in the distance they could hear seals barking.

"Oh, Ben, I feel so content."

Ben tightened his hold around Eva's waist. He saw her gentle smile. "It's fascinating out here."

Eva snuggled closer. "I love the fresh salt air and I just wish we could stay out here all day,"

A deck hand approached them. "We're asking everyone to return to their cars. We'll be docking soon." The tree topped mountains above Glasgow were approaching all too fast. Ben and Eva reluctantly returned to the coupe.

They drove off the ferry and onto a good gravel road. They drove north through the small town of

Hauser and seven miles later came to an abrupt stop at the town of Lakeside.

"Damn!" Ben said. "Another detour. Look at all that dust up ahead. Steam caterpillars and steam shovels, Phew! We'll never get through that mess." Along with the equipment were about fifty men working feverishly with picks and shovels. A workman approached them.

"Sorry," he said. "You'll have to use the beaches to get to Reedsport. This section of the Roosevelt Highway is under construction. We are requesting that everyone use the beach if they're going north."

"I want to see the foreman," Ben said. "We're reporters with the Portland *Oregonian* newspaper."

"That's him over there with the brown hat." The workman went to get the foreman and brought him back to the couple. Ben got out of his car to greet the man.

"Wait here," he told Eva.

"Hi. My name is Robert Potts, lead foreman for the state highway commission." He shook Ben's hand. "You're a reporter?"

"Yes. It's my job to write a report on the building of this highway from Crescent City to Astoria. Any information you can give me I'm sure would help.

"Since you're reporters I'll give you the grand tour. You're in luck because everyone else is being asked to take the beach to Reedsport. When we're finished you'll have learned how this portion of the highway is being constructed. It's typical of road construction on the entire highway. Get back into your car and I'll show you how a road is built."

After Ben returned to his seat, the foreman jumped on the running board. Robert waved to a man on a horse and motioned him to lead the small group.

"Follow that man on the horse," Robert said. "Hey,

Pete, get out of the way. We're coming through. This is the worst of it through this stretch. As you can see we've still got a lot of grading and leveling left."

Ben's coupe bumped along as he tried to listen to the foreman. It was hard to hear because of the ear-shattering steam engines at work.

Further on Robert pointed out, "Here's where the roadbed has already been laid. This is the most important part of any road and the most costly. We're bringing in crushed rock to provide the foundation for the fine gravel to be laid later. That's a rock-crushing machine up ahead on the right." Ben heard a loud grinding noise as boulders were dropped into the top and crushed into gravel. Ben thought Robert was doing a good job explaining the machinery and the stage of the highway's completion. Pott's had them stop numerous times so he could show them the plans and surveyor's maps indicating the route of the road. After a bumpy two hour drive through the work zone they finally reached Reedsport.

"Well, that's about it on this stretch of the Roosevelt," Robert said. "You'll find the road from Gardiner to Florence graded in places, but still very rough. Hope I was of help to you. Don't forget to spell my name correctly: Potts with two t's." Robert jumped off the running board. He and the horse rider headed off to a nearby café.

The trip with Potts had taken longer then expected. It was past one p.m. when Ben and Eva drove through Reedsport to the ferry dock on the south side of the Umpqua River. It took quite some time before the little five car ferry showed up. The ferry bumped and rocked its way into the landing. Three cars drove off.

"That'll be fifty cents, please," the ferry captain said. Ben paid the fifty cents and drove aboard. Two other cars joined them. Then off they went for another ferry ride. Once again Ben and Eva enjoyed the many sights and sounds while they crossed. From the ferry landing to the town of Gardiner the road was gravel. In Gardiner they stopped for gas.

"You've got a rough road ahead," the gas station attendant warned. "It hasn't been worked on for years."

"Thanks for the tip," Ben said. Soon they reached the notorious stretch of dirt road that would take them to Florence. It turned east towards the Coast Range. The coupe turned to the right and wobbled up a road that wasn't much more then a well-trodden cow path.

"Maybe someday there'll be more good roads like the one that connects Marshfield to Coquille," Eva mused. "This road is terrible." She was looking at her self in her little hand held mirror when the car hit a bump. The mirror smashed against the door. "Darn it! My mirror is broken," Eva exclaimed. Ben noticed that she had been trying to adjust her red hat. "Can you slow down a little bit?"

Ben braked to a stop. The car idled in neutral, Eva looking in a piece of the broken mirror to adjust her hat. "There that's better."

Ben let out the clutch and pressed the gas pedal, but before they could go a hundred yards the car ground to a halt.

"What the heck! The gas pedal is depressed but we aren't moving." Ben turned off the engine and got out. "Eva, you ought to look at this. The car is resting on the center of two deep ruts. The wheels aren't even touching the ground."

"Oh no," Eva moaned.

"Well, it's the same old routine," Ben said. "I'll shovel dirt. You cut some fir boughs." While Eva went off for the boughs Ben took a swig from his flask. Then, he started shoveling. The work took about two hours before they were able to move the car. Twenty minutes later they were stuck again and had to redo the procedure to get the car moving. Just when everything seemed to be going smooth the right rear tire blew.

"Why don't you hand me the tools while I work to replace the tire," Ben said. Another hour passed before they were driving again.

"What else can possibly go wrong?" Eva asked.

"Oh," Ben said. "Up ahead do you see them?" A large herd of cows was blocking the road.

After waiting for the cattle to get out of their way it was close to seven p.m. They finally reached the outskirts of Glenada, a little town on the south bank of the Siuslaw River. Thankfully, the ferry from Glenada to Florence was still in operation. They crossed over the river. On the bank of the river was a hotel. Exhausted, sweaty, and covered with dust, they rented a room. Immediately, they went to bed with out a meal.

It was early Saturday morning when they awoke. They were starving. They decided to eat breakfast at the café next to the hotel. It was a small place with a counter and two tables next to the window. Ben instantly liked the place. It smelled clean and there was a festive atmosphere inside. The owner greeted them at the door and invited them to take a seat. They chose a table by the window. Ben could see the sun just cresting the Coast Range. As the cook made their breakfast behind the counter he sang and whistled. It wasn't long before steaming plates of food were set down in front of them.

The cook pulled the curtains to shield them from the bright sun. "I know you're visitors from out of town. What type of work you do?"

"We're journalists with the Portland *Oregonian*."

Ben answered.

"Really?" the cook replied. "I know a story you should cover."

Both Eva and Ben put down their coffee cups and looked up at the man.

"What story?" Ben asked.

"My brother, Bill Stepps, owns oceanfront property about ten miles north of here. On his acreage is a Steller sea lion cave. He needs help keeping bounty hunters off his property. I was thinking that maybe if you were to write a story about his problem it might help him get government help." Ben saw that Eva looked concerned.

"Yes," Eva said. "I might like to write a story about that. How do we get in contact with your brother? I'd like to see the cave."

"I'll call him and have him waiting for you on the cliffs above the caves. He's the only one that should be there. Most people are afraid to go there because he chases them off with his rifle. Sometimes hunters come close to the cave in small boats from the sea and shoot the sea lions. But as long as my brother is up on the cliffs they stay clear. It's one thing to see sea lions stretched out on reefs, but it's even better to see them in that huge cavern. My brother wants to preserve their home. But I better warn you—climbing down to the caves is treacherous. People have died trying it."

"It sounds dangerous to me. I'm not much of a climber." Ben ate the last bite of crispy bacon.

"Oh, Ben, we have to go see them," Eva said eagerly. She gulped down her last drop of coffee.

"My brother will show you the easiest way to the cave." The cook said. "It's really safe if you follow his directions."

"Can we go there Ben?" Eva begged. "Please? I'll go alone if you don't. I want to see them."

"I'll go," Ben said reluctantly. They paid the cook. Then they drove north through the town of Florence. Their next stop would be the sea lions' cave. Eva was so excited she could hardly sit still.

Chapter Eighteen

Tom woke up Friday morning about seven. He was starved. He knelt on the bank of Coos Bay and scooped up water with cupped hands to wash his face. When he stood up, water dripped from his three-week-old beard. He looked out across the water. Sunlight fell on the white sails of a sloop loaded down with logs, slowly cruising out to sea. I've got to find them soon, he thought. If I don't, I risk losing my Eva forever. My first step is to find out how to get across this bay. He decided to find a café, eat breakfast, and then ask for directions to the ferry.

It wasn't long before he located a restaurant in downtown Marshfield. He went inside and sat at the counter. He could smell fresh donuts frying.

"Coffee?" the waitress asked.

"Black," Tom said. The waitress soon returned with a pot of coffee. She began filling his thick porcelain cup.

"How do I get to the ferry?" Tom asked.

"It's six blocks that way." She pointed north. "In a few minutes you'll be able to see the line of cars because it'll extend in front of my café. The people always come in here for coffee while they wait. If I were you I'd get your car in line as soon as you can." She put the coffeepot back on the burner.

Tom gulped down his coffee, paid for five fresh donuts, and rushed to his car. He could see cars lining up half a block away. He maneuvered forward until he joined the line.

He sat in his car wolfing down his donuts. Crumbs fell on his lap. When he finished he pondered his next move. So far his attempts to get Eva had failed. Unfortunately, he would have to rely on luck. Because of the highway's unpredictable condition, there were detours, muddy roads, and ferries. He figured eventually those very features would aid him. Soon Eva and Ben would have a stretch of bad luck too. That's when he'd overtake them.

Three hours later he was across the bay and driving north. He passed through Hauser and by noon he reached Lakeside and the road building zone. Detour signs pointed to the west but Tom drove straight toward the gravel piles, workmen, and horse drawn graders.

The same man who had stopped Ben and Eva suddenly appeared in front of Tom with his hand held up. "Sorry bud." He said. "This road is closed for construction. You'll have to use the detour we've set up. It's that way."

"You don't understand!" Tom said impatiently. "I have to get through. It's an emergency. My brother is on his death bed. It's a matter and life and death."

"Sorry to hear that about your brother, mister, but there's nothing I can do. Earlier we could have taken you through, but not now. The road's blocked up ahead. The quickest way to get to Reedsport is to take the detour." He pointed to a gravel road leading off to the west. "Follow it until you come to a plank road. That will lead you to the beach. The beach will take you to Winchester Bay. We hired a scow that will take you from there to Reedsport. Good luck."

Tom had no choice. Angrily, he sped off on the gravel road. When he reached the planked road he knew he was going in the right direction. His car bounced, and rocked as he drove over the uneven surface. The road extended out onto the sand. Thankfully the tide was out.

"Good," he said to himself. "I'll be able to make good time here." He zoomed along the beach at 30 or 40 miles an hour. The salt air filled his lungs. The green forest stretched to his right, and the beautiful blue of the Pacific Ocean stretched to his left. Everything was going well until he reached a rather large creek draining into the ocean.

I'll just follow the stream until it narrows enough to drive across, he thought. He found a narrower spot and crossed. Once on the other side, the sand was so soft his tires sank up to the hub caps. The harder he pressed down on the gas, the deeper he sank. No matter what he tried, in first gear or reverse, he couldn't drive his car out of the sand. What can I do now? He thought in frustration. Off in the distance he saw a logging camp. Maybe they can help, he thought. He got out of the sedan and trudged through the soft sand, kicking seashells, as he went.

"I need help getting my car free of the sand," Tom told one of the workmen.

"There's nothing we can do. The foreman is off in the woods and won't be back until this evening."

"I'm willing to pay anyone who will help me," Tom said. He pulled out a wad of cash and showed it to the man.

"Frank, come over here," the workman yelled. Frank sauntered over. "Listen, do you think we can use the horses to pull this gent's car out of the sand?" He winked. "He's willing to pay us. The boss will never know."

"I don't know," Frank said. "How much are you willing to pay, mister?"

"Ten dollars," Tom said desperately.

"We might lose our jobs doing this, and we might

take a beating from the boss besides," Frank said. "I'll tell you what, make it twenty and we'll go get the horses."

"I'll give you fifteen and that's all."

"I'm sorry to hear that, mister. Toby, let's get back to work."

"Okay. Twenty it is," Tom said with a sigh.

The men took their time putting reins on the horses and leading them to Tom's car; so it was late afternoon by the time he finally got to Winchester Bay. He found the old scow standing by for detoured cars.

"Do you need a lift into Reedsport?" The scow operator asked Tom.

"Why else would I be here?" Tom snorted.

The old man helped him maneuver the vehicle onto the scow. With a long pole the man pushed off from the sand, and the incoming tide helped move the raft towards Reedsport.

"Oh, my gosh!" the man said. Water had started creeping into the scow. Already it was almost ankle deep.

"Will I ever have a stretch of good luck?" Tom said disgustedly. "I wish I could just get my car to a real road!"

"Here's a bucket. Start bailing!" The old man ordered. So Tom and the old man bailed. The craft slowly made its way east towards a small dock. Just off the dock was a passable road that led into Reedsport. Once off the sinking old tub, Tom drove to Reedsport and the ferry landing at the edge of the Umpqua River. It was eight thirty p.m. and night was settling in. He had to search through town to locate the ferry operator.

"After seven p.m. the rates go up," the ferry captain said.

"How much," Tom asked, losing his patience.

"Two dollars."

Tom paused, looking at the man. What else could he do? It was important that he keep moving, especially now since the fiasco on the sand. So he pulled out his wallet and paid the additional night fee. I can't believe it, he thought, after the ferry actually crossed the river without a delaying incident.

North of the Umpqua River the next town he came to was the lumber community of Gardiner. He stopped at the only gas pump he could find. It was in front of a small grocery store. A light above the door revealed a sign *Ring bell for night service*. It was only nine thirty p.m. so Tom hoped the owner was still awake. He got out of his car and rang the bell. The store owner soon came out of the door.

"I want my gas tank filled," Tom ordered. The attendant dispensed the gas. Tom paid the man and climbed back in the car. "By the way, I'm trying to catch up with some friends of mine, a man and woman about my age. They're in a Buick coupe going north too. Have you seen them?"

"They came through hours ago. You're a long ways behind them. And if you think you can follow tonight, forget it. The road ahead is barely passable even in daylight."

Tom wasn't about to stop now. Traveling by night was the only way to make up for lost time. Once out of town, his head lamps lit up a crude sign, with an arrow pointing north, *31 miles to Florence*. The moon darted behind some clouds. Tom's sedan bumped along in the darkness. He could just make out the outline of a forest against the night sky. Before long the dark, giant trees were overhead. Moss hung from the branches and slid across the car. The glow of the head lamps reflected off orange animal eyes, staring at him from all sides. About ten miles out of Gardiner, Tom's car got high centered and the tires spun wildly. He noticed lights from a farmhouse in the distance.

The night was so quiet he could hear his footsteps crunch as he walked towards the house. Overhead an owl hooted. It was almost midnight when Tom reached the front door. He was very tired and very angry. He knocked on the door. The sudden noise made a cat bolt out of nearby bushes. Freighted, Tom turned quickly in the cat's direction. When he saw it was just a cat he turned back to the house and knocked again, louder this time.

"Okay, I'm coming," a voice said from inside the house. A man in his pajamas opened the door.

"What the—?" He stared at the revolver in Tom's hand.

"I need your horses to pull my car out about a mile back. So get them reined up pronto!" Tom ordered the old farmer. He followed the old man back to his bedroom to change clothes. Then Tom followed him to the barn where he reined up two white mares.

Tom pointed with his gun. "That way, and hurry."

After the horses had pulled the car back to a drivable part of the road, Tom asked, "How much farther to Florence?"

"About 20 miles, it's dry but still treacherous. You'll have to be careful not to get centered again. And you can put that gun down, mister; I'm not going to do anything."

Tom stuck the gun in his belt. The old man turned and led his horses away towards his home.

Tom thought about all the hardships he'd gone through to get this far. He had failed to get Eva at the hotel. He had missed Ben when shooting at him. Those idiots who ran the ferries slowed him down. He'd been robbed by two loggers. Then, he had to endure that ridiculous scow that almost sank. And, now, he'd been high centered on this rotten road. What's next? Then he thought of the old man. As soon as the farmer got back to his house he'd probably call the police. That was the last thing Tom needed. With a weary sigh Tom pulled his gun from his belt.

Just then the old man turned back for a last look at Tom. Tom raised the gun and saw the fear in the old man's eyes. The farmer began backing up as fast as his old legs would carry him.

"No more mishaps," Tom said. "No more idiots trying to stop me from getting my Eva. You won't be able to tell anyone when I'm through with you." Tom fired off two rounds into the old man's chest. Tom watched as the codger slumped to the ground, dead before he hit the dirt.

Tom dragged the body into the woods. He shooed the horses away, got back into his car and slowly drove off. The car bumped and bounced along. Tom drove cautiously for the rest of the night. It was dawn, Saturday morning, when he pulled into the small town of Glenada. Looking north Tom saw the Siuslaw River flowing steadily out to sea.

At Glenada's ferry landing he saw the Florence ferryboat across the river at the dock. He took out his telescope. Maybe they'd open for business soon, he thought. While scanning the landing with his scope he noticed Ben's car parked in front of the hotel. His lips formed into a sinister smile. At last, I've caught up with them. If only that darn ferry would come across now, he thought. While he stood there he spied Ben and Eva going into a small café. About twenty minutes later he saw them getting into the coupe and driving north.

Just then, he noticed the ferry loading cars. It was preparing to come across the river.

Chapter Nineteen

Ben and Eva turned off on the rutted road that led to the sea lion caves. They climbed a mountain thick with old Douglas fir trees. The car dipped into a swale, only to rise again and enter a forest of spruce and alder as they neared the coastal cliffs. They came down a hillside and drove out onto a headland. Ben parked the car. They got out and walked to the edge of a cliff that had a grand ocean view.

"Don't get to close to the edge," Eva said.

Ben stopped short of the cliff and Eva moved up next to him. Ben put his arm around Eva's shoulders.

"What a view," she said. Gulls soared up from the cliff's edge. "Don't you wish you could fly with those gulls? How thrilling it would be!" The blue, placid ocean stretched to the horizon. The wind whipped around them as Eva's arm draped around Ben's hips.

"Look there's a whale!" Eva exclaimed, pointing out to sea. Ben saw a spout of water blow up into the air. Then a huge tail slapped the water. Eva turned, her face, smiling, and looked into Ben's eyes. Their lips came together. Ben couldn't hear the seagulls, feel the wind, or even see the clouds that passed over head. After a long moment their lips parted.

"Eva," Ben said. "Sometimes I think I'm not good enough for you."

"Listen, Ben. I see something in you that you don't. I see a man who's more courageous then anyone I've ever met. If anything, I'm not good enough for you."

They kissed again.

"Ah-hem," said a voice behind them.

Ben and Eva quickly parted and turned around.

"I'm Bill Stepps, the owner of this property. You folks must be the reporters." A youngish man with a wide brimmed hat and a long brown beard was resting a rifle in the crook of his arm.

"Oh—sorry," Ben said, embarrassed. "How did you know we were reporters?"

"My brother called from town. I guess he told you I'm the owner of this unique piece of land. My property includes a sea lion cave, unlike any other in the world! The cave is the reason I bought this place."

Eva pulled out a writing pad. "Why are people slaughtering these sea lions?"

"For the bounty."

"You mean the government pays sea lion hunters?" Eva asked amazed.

"Yup," Bill replied. "Five dollars for every sea lion killed."

"That explains the slaughter we saw at Cape Blanco," Eva said.

"It's pretty grim, alright," Bill said. "The hunters shoot them, and stab them, behead them, whatever. Then they leave the bloody remains to rot on the rocks. All they take is just a flipper and that's just for proof of a kill so they can get their bounty from the county office."

"Why does the county allow this senseless slaughter?" Eva asked.

"The county commissioners claim the sea lions are eating too many salmon. There's no sense to it because there's plenty of salmon. The sea lions mostly don't eat salmon anyway, just trash fish, crabs, and scraps."

"I think," Eva said, "that the salmon are more threatened by man than by sea lions."

"That's the truth. I've seen the population of this cave colony dwindle considerably since that senseless law was enacted."

"I thought so," Eva put her note pad in a pocket.

Ben was trying to stay noncommittal. He felt that if the laws were locally enacted then there must have been other reasons.

"How do we get down to the cave?" Eva asked.

"I'll show you the way down from here. You'll have to be extremely careful.

"I don't know, Eva," Ben said. "Should we do this?"

"We'll take it slow, real slow," Eva said.

"You'll make it. Just be careful and watch your step," Bill said. "Unfortunately, I have to stay here because I don't want hunters on my land. Now, just follow that path off to the left. It'll zigzag down the slope and lead you to the mouth of a large cave. Be careful!"

Ben and Eva began the descent down the hill.

Chapter Twenty

Tom got back into his car, to wait for the ferry. He was tired after the long night's drive. No matter how hard he tried, Tom couldn't keep his eyes open. He nodded off into a deep sleep. But he woke up with a start when the ferry bumped into pilings at the Glenada landing dock. The captain dropped the chain and three cars drove ashore. Then the captain motioned for Tom to drive aboard. Tom started up his engine and carefully drove onto the ferry. He was the only car this trip.

Once on the other side of the Siuslaw River he followed a road that had recently been graveled. For a few miles he thought it was going to be easy going. Unfortunately, the road turned rugged as it wound its way up into the Coast Range. He was about four miles up the narrow road when he noticed a big car approaching. He had seen stages like this before in the Willamette valley. Expanded cars, they were used to transport passengers from one town to another. Tom thought: He's going to have to back up and let me by. I won't stand for another delay. Both vehicles approached each other slowing to a stop with their front fenders almost touching. Tom angrily got out of his car, slammed his door, and walked toward the stage.

The stage driver got out too. The two men met between the cars.

"Get this contraption out of my way," Tom snarled.

"Sir, I've driven this road many times," the coach

driver replied. "This is the first time a driver has not immediately backed up and found a turnoff, to let me by. I'm delivering people and mail to Florence and I have the right-of-way. Start backing up now."

"The rules of the road say the driver going up the hill has the right-of-way."

"That rule is for cars, not for stages, you idiot. Now back up!"

"You get out of my way!" Tom snapped.

People were hanging out the windows of the stage. "What's happening up there Charles? Why won't that stranger back up?"

"Time's running out mister. Back up or we'll back you up. I don't want to get the sheriff involved in this. It's up to you."

Seeing he had no other choice, Tom returned grudgingly to his car and began backing up. By the time he found a turnoff he had reached the good road that led back to Florence. The stage roared past him, leaving dust so thick Tom's car nearly disappeared from view. Another stupid delay, Tom thought.

He drove back up the rutted road until he came to the side road that led to the caves. One arrow pointed west to the sea lion caves and another arrow pointed north to Yachats. Tom drove west. About two miles later he noticed a no trespassing sign. Tom got out and checked the road. Aw, he thought, just as I had expected, fresh tire tracks. I couldn't have planned for a better ambush site.

He started the engine and slowly drove past the sign.

"Wham!!" A bullet shattered the front lower louvered windowpane and smashed into his passenger car seat with a thud.

"Goddamn it!" Tom yelled. He quickly put his car in reverse and backed up as fast as the car would go.

Another shot whizzed above his car and smacked into a large spruce. He backed behind some shrubbery and got out. From behind a tree he used his spy glass to look up the hill. He saw Bill standing there with his rifle. He also saw the rear end of Ben's parked car. He saw Bill shoot another shot in the air. That crazy galoot, I've got to get out of here, he thought. He had to back all the way to the road that led to Yachats. He was badly shaken. He knew Eva was at the caves but he didn't dare go out there with someone shooting at him. He decided to move ahead of them and ambush them further up the road.

Tom drove slowly north over the rutted lane looking for another ambush site. As he drove along he thought about what had happened back home. The thing he couldn't understand was why his mother had tried to stop him from getting back with Eva.

"Leave her alone," Ma had yelled at him in a drunken slur. "She doesn't want to see you. What did you do to make her mad at you? Did you hit her? You did, didn't you?" His mother slapped him. That's when he lost his temper and everything went blank. When he recovered he realized with horror that he'd strangled her. Actually, killing Ma was an accident, he thought. Since his mother was dead he knew his father would have to die too. His father wouldn't have understood. Tom felt he had no choice. So he shot his father when he came through the front door.

If my Eva had only married me as we had planned, none of this would have happened, he thought. Her deceit led me to kill my parents. It all seemed so logical.

Tom was deep in thought as his Ford wound around Cape Perpetua on a road that clung to a perilous cliff high above the pacific breakers.

Chapter Twenty-one

Ben and Eva slowly, ever so slowly, clambered down the precipitous cliff to the sea lion caves. They reached a small creek that tumbled down the slope. Ben leapt to the other side.

"Take my hand, Eva," Ben said. If either of them were to slip they'd fall hundreds of feet to the crashing surf below. Eva reached for his hand and jumped.

"Whew!" Eva said as she cleared the rushing water.

Some rocks had scraped loose during the jump and bounced down the cliff. Ben and Eva inched along the narrow path. It seemed like ages before Eva spotted the mouth of the cave. "Ben, do you see it?"

"Yes. Listen!

"That must be the barking of the sea lions," Eva said. They entered through the gaping hole and slowly descended to a rocky floor. The narrow passageway was dimly lit and it took a while for their eyes to adjust. However there was enough light for Ben to see Eva pinch her nose. "Phew! I hope the sea lions look better than they smell."

When their eyes were fully adjusted, they ventured deeper into the cave. Their feet searched for flat surfaces. They braced themselves by holding their hands on either side of the tunnel.

"I can see sunlight down there," Eva said. "It's getting brighter. Look, it opens up to the sea."

The narrow passage suddenly opened into a cavernous area. They could see the waves washing in to form a gigantic pool completely inside the cave. This was where all the noise had come. Waves crashed and sea lions barked like a deranged pack of wolves.

"Let's sit on these rocks," Ben shouted above the noise. One of the big male sea lions threatened to charge them, but then changed his mind and scooted back to the herd. Ben and Eva sat on a rock watching the spectacle. Below them the giant pool rose and fell with the waves and the tide. A large rock jutting up from the center of the pool seemed to be a special sea lion perch. When waves crashed on it, sea lions would leap from the water to gain a footing.

Sea lions crowded around the cave's rocky edge. The males tried to gain vantage points hoping to attract the females. As they barked and fought for the highest position they glared at their rivals with dark eyes and lifted their whiskered noses threateningly. When they had won their slippery perch, they strutted around on two fins, bellowing in barks of triumph.

Ben and Eva sat spellbound. This was a timeless sanctuary. Ben felt that he and Eva were lucky indeed to have found such a place. He put his arm around her. Her face turned toward him. He couldn't resist and kissed her. It was a long and sensuous kiss. Their rapture led to a world where time and place weren't important. When their kiss ended, Ben kissed Eva on the ear and neck, and Eva kissed Ben gently on the forehead.

"Well what do you two think about my cave?" Bill said as Ben and Eva came over the cliff's edge.

"There's an incredible story here," Eva answered. "I want to write an article about protecting the sea lions."

"We appreciate you letting us go down there," Ben said. "It was a great experience."

"Feel free to come back anytime. I just wish there

were more people like you who'd come here and enjoy this special place without trying to harm the sea lions. I'll look for your newspaper article, Eva."

With this wonderful experience behind them the two drove back to the highway that would take them north to Yachats.

"This is the worst road we've been on," Ben said. "I'm just glad it's not raining or we'd never make it through." The coupe clambered over rocks and deep ruts as they slowly rattled on. At one moment they were driving next to the beach. The next moment they were in a rain forest crossing creeks on little wooden bridges. Later, they drove a narrow rock ledge around Cape Perpetua, hundreds of feet above the pounding surf. Not much was said as Ben slowly drove around the cape, a stone wall on their right and a steep drop-off to their left. A sharp corner loomed ahead.

"Careful, Ben," Eva cautioned.

Ben slowed to make the curve. Ahead they saw a car parked in the middle of the road. Ben had to brake to a stop. "Oh, shit!!" Ben exclaimed.

Tom was getting out of the parked car with a pistol in his hand.

"Get down!" Eva shouted. "He's going to shoot!" Tom began to raise his pistol. Then he suddenly shoved the gun under his shirt.

"What the—?" Ben said, puzzled. "He's getting back in his car."

From behind Ben's coupe came the joyous shouts of passengers as the stage came around the perilous corner and stopped. The driver got out, furious that Tom was blocking the road again. "You again! Get moving, now!"

Tom's car lurched forward and slowly moved ahead.

"I'm reporting that guy to the sheriff when we get into Newport," Charles said. "Are you folks all right?"

"We're fine. Thank you," Ben said, as he watched Charles return to the stage.

"That was close," Eva said.

"We'll be safe as long as the stage is behind us," Ben said. "We'll just follow Tom to Yachats."

The caravan of two cars and the Studebaker stage dusted the hillside as they drove to the town of Yachats. Ben saw Tom's sedan turn off into a driveway to let the cars pass.

After Yachats, Ben drove ahead of the stage. The road led down onto the beach. They sped along the sand to Waldport. In Waldport, the stage stopped to let its passengers out. Ben and Eva proceeded alone on a rough road that led to the ferry landing on the south side of the Alsea River. Once across the River they were dumped on a sandy landing. They drove up a ramp to a wooden trestle road that rose above the sand on pilings.

"Eva, look, no hands," Ben said holding his hands in the air.

"Careful! We'll fall off this trestle," Eva admonished. Ben didn't have to steer because wood flanges in the middle of the trestle kept the car going straight. The raised wooden road led to the beach. With the tide out, Ben made very good time speeding over the sand to Yaquina Bay. Fortunately the ferry was just landing.

"Great, what luck!" Ben said. "We can hop on this ferry and be further ahead of Tom."

Chapter Twenty-two

They drove from the ferry landing into the bustling town of Newport. "If they have a police office here I want to talk with the sheriff," Eva said.

The sheriff's office was one of the first buildings they came to. Ben parked in front of it.

"We'd like to file a report about a man who is trying to kill us," Eva told the desk sergeant. The sergeant handed her a report form and went to fetch the sheriff. While Eva filled out the form, Ben took the sheriff outside and showed him the bullet hole in the car door.

"The driver of the stage will be here soon," Ben said. "I think he wants to fill out a report too."

By the time they went back inside the office, Eva had completed the form. After looking at the completed report the sheriff said, "I'll be on the lookout for him."

"Good. Where can we find the *Newport Sentinel* office?" Ben asked.

"It's on Main Street, three blocks up the road on the right hand side. You can't miss it."

Five minutes later, Ben and Eva were driving into the driveway of an old house that had been converted into the newspaper office. When the door clanged shut behind them they found themselves in a large un-partitioned room. There were two desks in the front and newspaper presses in the back. One man was setting type for the presses and another was going through stacks of paper at one of the desks.

The man at the desk looked up as Ben and Eva entered the room. "What can I do for you?"

"We're reporters from the *Oregonian*. My name is Ben Cooper and this is Eva Barton. I'm looking for information about the Roosevelt Highway."

"You came to the right place. My name is Stanley Buckman, I'm the editor. Why, only yesterday there was a big organizational meeting of businesses from Astoria to Crescent City right here in Newport. We're trying to organize all of the coastal towns in a publicity campaign."

"A publicity campaign?" Ben asked. "You mean about the Roosevelt Highway?"

"That's right. We want to tell the world about the accommodations, natatoriums, camping sites, and of course the spectacular beauty along this route. We're hoping tourists will come to see this scenic wonderland. We have to promote this area and at the same time encourage our state legislators to keep funding highway construction. Our meeting was a resounding success, and the legislators that were here promised to do everything in their power to get the job of building the highway done as soon as possible."

Stanley looked at Eva and asked, "Are you writing about the highway too?"

"My stories will deal more with conservation issues. I'm planning one article about the Steller sea lions. I think these poor defenseless animals are being slaughtered for no practical purpose."

"I remember reading an article you wrote not too long ago about the forests east of here. You suggested that the logging company keep a swath of trees along side the roads, didn't you?" Eva said

"That's right, Eva," Stanley said. "If you hide the acres and acres where the trees have all been cut down it would be more inviting for the tourist to travel through here. That article has caused me a lot of grief, and even a few personal attacks. It's not worth the loss of my paper to try and persuade the largest logging company in the world to change the way they do business. This paper is my livelihood. Around here we're all dependent on the logging industry. Still, I admire Jess and you for your courage. It takes guts for Jess to allow articles like that in his paper."

"Jess has published four of my letters," Eva said proudly. "He's sent me along with Ben to write more. Jess is a good friend of my father. They both belong to the organization trying to save the redwoods. My father has convinced me that the Oregon forests are just as important and pristine as the redwoods. I just wish I could convince Ben how we think. He's the best writer on the *Oregonian* staff.

Ben noticed out of the corner of his eye that the pressman was walking over to the table.

"Mr. Buckman, here are three issues of Wednesday's paper. Your guests might be interested in reading a copy. It has the full text of what happened at the Roosevelt Highway Association meeting yesterday."

Eva and Ben began to read the front page.

"Ben?" Eva said.

"I see it," Ben said. On the front page was a picture of Tom. The article below the photo told about his parent's death and noted that Tom was wanted for questioning.

"He's really snapped," Eva said. "I'm sure he killed his parents. Now he wants to kill us. His life is virtually over. The only thing keeping him going is his pursuit of us."

The editor's ears perked up. "Are you two involved with the killer? Now there's a story I'd like to print. What's happened?"

Eva told Stanley about how Tom had been stalking them and attempting to kill them.

Meanwhile Ben noticed another article staring him in the face.

PACIFIC SPRUCE CORPORATION HONORS CAFETERIA COOK

Rosa Cooper will be given a generous Award tomorrow for her dedicated service managing the cafeteria at the mill. The food has always been excellent including stews, fried chicken, Pies, and much, much more. The corporation owners plan on giving her a generous cash bonus. The ceremony Will be Sunday at 2 p.m.

"What is it, Ben?" Eva asked.

"I'm not entirely sure," Ben said, his face beaming. "This cook at the big spruce mill in Toledo is being honored tomorrow. Her name is Rosa Cooper, the same as my mother. It makes me wonder. Do you know anything about this woman, Stanley?"

"The only thing I know is that she's been there for about eighteen years. She's the best cook in the county."

"Eighteen years?" Ben said with growing excitement. "Then there's a chance she really might be my mother." He told Stanley about how his mother had had smallpox and had left him with friends. The friends had put him in an orphanage with a note on his jacket explaining how his mother had been dying.

"I've heard of recoveries from smallpox. It's entirely possible your mother is the cook. What a story that would make!" Stanley slapped his hand on the desk. "Listen, why don't you folks stay with me tonight? First thing tomorrow morning, after church, we'll go to the mill and see if she is your mother. If she is, then we'll have a very special reunion at that award ceremony. What do you say?"

"Let's do it Ben," Eva said.

"Okay, I'll do it, but what about Tom?" Ben asked.

"Don't you folks worry about Tom. He'll never find you at my place, and we can hide your car in my garage. Besides, it will give me time to find out more about Tom Bigalow. I want to print a follow up article on him right away. The man's a murderer. Maybe the public can help locate him. It puzzles me why the Coos Bay Times didn't print the story."

"The Coos Bay editor was pretty mad at us when we left his office," Ben said.

"Sam's pretty tight with the mill owners," Stanley replied, lowering his eyebrows. "Believe me, your story will be out in my paper this Wednesday."

"May I keep this issue of your paper?" Ben Asked. "The information about the Roosevelt Highway Association meeting will help me write my article."

"Absolutely!" Stanley said. He turned to Eva, "When we go to the spruce mill I'd be very careful what you say. That mill supports a lot of people. The owners get nervous when someone starts talking about saving the big trees. Now it's getting late, so let's get out of here and go over to my house."

Blakely

Kidnapped

Chapter Twenty-three

Tom slowly drove out onto the main road and into the town of Yachats. From Yachats he took the road that led to the beach. While traveling over the hard, damp sand, he worried about coming up with a plan. It was turning out to be almost impossible to plan a kidnapping when Ben and Eva were constantly moving from town to town. Surely somewhere along this route he'd be presented with the opportunity he was looking for. Be patient, he thought: your time will come.

Tom passed through Waldport and crossed the Alsea River on the ferry. Once again he returned to the beach, this time headed for Newport. The tide was out, but he could hear the waves as they crashed on the sand. Tiny birds scampered in groups at the water's edge.

About midway to Newport, Tom saw an abandoned car mired in the sand. No one was around, so he stopped. Tom figured that the authorities were probably on the lookout for him by now. He needed to change his identity. The screws on the abandoned car's license plate were rusty and the job took longer than he wanted. "Finally!" He whispered as the screws came off. Then he unscrewed his own license plates and made the change.

He found an old brown felt hat on the back seat of the car. "Perfect!" He said. And he tried it on. The brim folded down sharply. It not only covered his curly black hair but a large portion of his forehead as well. Combined with his growing beard and general shabbiness, this new addition to his appearance might help him remain undetected a little longer.

It was early evening when he reached Yaquina Bay. He decided to wait until dark before crossing to Newport on the ferry. Once on the ferry Tom noticed the captain writing down his license plate number. He immediately tensed up, yet he knew he had to act casual. He got out of his car and walked over to a man standing at the rail.

"We're in luck, it's not raining," Tom said. A waxing moon lit the sky and Tom could see the ripples of water flowing away from the ferry as they cruised along.

"It's not much fun riding this ferry when it's raining," the man said. "Not much fun driving to the mill either."

"What mill is that?"

"You must be new around here," the man said. "It's the biggest lumber mill in the world. It's called the Toledo Spruce Lumber Mill. They give tours. You should go through it if you get the chance. I work there as a sawyer."

"I've heard that's one of the highest paid jobs," Tom said.

"I'm paid well. If you decide to take the tour tell them at the front office that Tim Collins told you to come. Just about every tourist takes the tour, but you'll get special treatment." The words echoed in Tom's mind. Everyone goes through the mill, he thought. Eva wouldn't miss the opportunity and neither would Ben.

"What's the road like to the mill?" Tom said.

"It's good gravel," Tim said. "You could camp between Newport and Toledo. There's a sign just off the ferry landing that directs you to the road. It's easy to find."

When Tom drove from the ferry landing into

Newport he felt a little better. The ferryboat captain seemed to have lost interest in him. He knew he had to be cautious. Good thing his car wasn't the only Ford sedan on the road, he thought.

Tom spotted the Toledo road sign easily, just like Tim had said, and drove east towards the mill. He felt certain Ben and Eva would go that way too. Right now, however, the road was deserted. Thanks to the moon he saw a narrow dirt lane that turned off alongside a creek. He left the gravel road, and squeezed his car between two huge Sitka spruce trees, and followed the creek for a short distance. The car was completely hidden from the road. He left his head lamps on while he built a fire. After he turned off his head lamps he sat on the running board of his Ford. He drank from his flask while the fire crackled and hissed before him. He saw the flames shoot up in the air and disappear in the darkness. He could hear the creek as it splashed over rocks dashing towards the Yaquina River. The moon had slipped behind some clouds.

He felt lonely for the first time. How he missed being with his Eva! She'd love this place with the creek and big trees. We could be enjoying this together if only she'd stay with me. I still feel the soft touch of her hand and the passion of her lips, he thought. The irises of his eyes reflected the wild antics of the fire. The more he drank the sadder he became. He abruptly stood up and yelled into the emptiness, "I want my Eva back!"

He gathered up some cedar boughs and spread them out on the ground next to the car. Next he spread his blanket on top. He felt very tired as he lay on the soft bed. He peered up at the stars intermingled with the ancient tree tops and drifted off to sleep. The night passed and the fire slowly turned to embers and finally to ash.

At dawn he built another fire and prepared some

coffee. He pulled out a cigarette and lit it. When the coffee was ready he filled his tin cup. Then he set the cup on the running board and examined his gun. Satisfied that the chamber was loaded, he aimed the gun at a tree. The shot rang out as the bullet dug into the bark. His ears rang from the loud blast. He reloaded his gun and shoved it under his belt. He finished his cigarette and coffee, got up, and kicked dirt over the fire.

The light of morning slowly began to penetrate the forest canopy. He hoped that Ben and Eva had stayed in a Newport hotel and would come along the road soon. He ran his hand through his hair as he weighed how best to ambush them. He noticed a huge old spruce stump between two gigantic firs. If he sat next to the stump it would give him a hidden vantage point for watching the road. He prepared a soft site on the ground and sat down. He pulled the gun from his belt and rested his arm on the stump. He aimed into the forest across the road. Tom's finger tightened on the trigger. Wham! And a bullet screamed into the forest. Aw, this will work fine, he thought. Then he hunched over, relaxed, and waited.

Chapter Twenty-four

Ben, Eva, and Stanley, the editor, sat in the modest kitchen of a small home not too far from the newspaper office. Mrs. Frances Buckman, white haired and skinny, stood over the woodstove cooking blueberry flapjacks. A pot of coffee percolated, steaming a refreshing smell into the room. A gentle breeze ruffled the curtains. The orange light of morning danced on the walls and floor. Fragments of food on sticky plates showed that breakfast was almost over.

"We've had enough, Frances," Stanley said. "No more pancakes please."

"Yes, I'm stuffed," Ben confirmed. "Please, no more for me."

"Come sit down and eat something," Eva urged Mrs. Buckman.

Frances piled two pancakes on her plate and swiftly sat down in the remaining empty chair. She poured hot maple syrup over them. Her fork sliced through the pancake and clinked on the plate. She speared the severed section, and then shoved the morsel in her mouth.

Stanley took a sip of coffee then replaced the cup on the saucer.

"As soon as Frances finishes eating and we clean up the kitchen we'll all drive to church in my car. After church we'll go out to the mill." Everyone agreed that it was a good plan. When Francis finished, Eva and the men got up to help wash the dishes.

The foursome went to church in Stanley's sedan and returned home about eleven a.m. Because Ben and Eva would be traveling north after seeing the mill, the two couples decided to take separate cars.

"I want Eva to ride with me because I want to find out more about Tom," Stanley said. "Ben, you can fill Frances in about your mother." Eva got into Stanley's car and Frances got into Ben's. It was twelve-thirty when they headed off for the mill.

Forty-five minutes later, the two cars topped a rise in the gravel road. Ben's mouth dropped open. Sprawled before him was the largest lumber mill in the world. The steam stacks of the main sawmill building towered upwards a hundred feet. At least twenty huge buildings were spread out across acres of land. Some of the buildings were open sheds for drying stacked lumber. A large wigwam burner, next to the main mill, spewed white smoke that stood out against the steely grey clouds. A man-made canal stretched the entire length of the operation, and, in the canal, logs drifted between pilings and log-rafts. Most of the nearby hills had been stripped of their trees. Only tall snags and stumps remained. Steam rose from the bare ground. Because Sunday was a day of rest, the mill lay dormant, peaceful, inviting, and intriguing.

Ben followed Stan's car into the heart of the compound. Stan parked in front of a long, single-story building. The word *cafeteria* stood over the front door. Ben parked his coupe alongside Stan's car.

A crowd of workmen had gathered outside the entrance, dressed in logging boots, plaid shirts, and suspenders. Greeting everyone at the door was Mr. Gordon, one of the mill's owners. When Stanley and Frances entered, Mr. Gordon grabbed Stanley's hand and pulled him to the side. He complemented him on one of his recent articles in the *Sentinel*.

"Who are your friends?" Mr. Gordon asked.

"This is Ben Cooper and Eva Barton. They're reporters from the *Oregonian*."

"Well, well," Mr. Gordon said. "Please take those seats for VIPs up at the front tables."

"I have some interesting news for you," Stanley said.

"What is it?" Mr. Gordon said, wanting to get on with his greetings.

"Mr. Cooper might be Rosa Cooper's son."

"What!" Mr. Gordon said. "Good God! Are you serious?"

"I'm really not sure," Ben said quickly. "Has Rosa ever talked about a son?"

"She has indeed, on many occasions, Mr. Gordon said. "Rosa lost contact with him when he was a baby because she had smallpox. She was never able to find out what happened to him."

"Well!" Ben said beaming. "She's got to be Mother, then. Amazing! The whole story about her smallpox was written on a note that was pinned to my shirt when I was taken into the orphanage. I want to see her, right away."

"Wait a minute, young man. Let's make something special of this reunion. I have an idea. Listen, when I present her with her cash bonus, I'll also introduce you. Let's reunite you in front of the audience. It will be a special moment she'll remember for the rest of her life. What do you say?"

"Ben, you have to say yes," Eva said.

"Alright. What do you want me to do, Mr. Gordon?"

"Your mother is sitting at the far end of the head table."

Ben looked nervously in his mother's direction. He knew she was his mother at once. Ben could see her bright blue eyes under graying blond hair. She was pleasantly plump with an oval face and red cheeks. She has a wonderful presence, an engaging smile, Ben thought, overwhelmed with pride.

"I want you to sit at the other end of the table next to me," Mr. Gordon said. "After I've given her the bonus check, you stand up and start walking towards us. That's when I'll spring the surprise on her. This is going to be terrific! Stanley could even write a nice article about the event in his paper. Let's go take our seats."

Mr. Gordon led Ben up to the front table. His mother smiled at him as he approached. When he sat down he couldn't help thinking to himself. At last, a reunion with his mother! He could hardly wait. He didn't even care that Mr. Gordon was making a big show of it. The important thing was to finally meet her.

White table cloths covered the big tables that filled the big hall. Silverware, plates, and glasses had been placed in readiness for the upcoming meal. In the middle of the tables were big bowls of steaming food. The crowd waited until Mr. Gordon gave the go ahead, then elbows, hands, and forks dove into the meal. Soon, only remnants of food remained on the plates in front of half-filled coffee cups.

Mr. Gordon rose and approached the podium at the center of the table. "Before we get to our special event, I'd like to give out some awards. We've spared nothing to provide you with the finest and safest equipment. Under the leadership of John Smith and Jim Albers, the implementation and use of our new equipment has resulted in the last three months being accident free. So, if John and Jim would come forward I would like to give them certificates of appreciation." Modest applause greeted the two as they walked to the head table. Mr. Gordon handed them their certificates.

"Please stay here while I make the next presentation. It has also come to my attention that Frank Arbuckle has done a fantastic job implementing fire safety procedures. Frank, please come forward for your certificate." Again, there was modest applause. Mr. Gordon then dismissed them.

"And now for our special event," Mr. Gordon said. "As most of you know, this luncheon is to celebrate a lady who has shown outstanding character and professionalism." People began applauding and cheering even before Rosa's name was mentioned. How proud this made Ben feel! His eyes grew damp, his hands shook, at the thought that he was about to meet his mother.

"All right," Mr. Gordon said, holding up his hands to quiet the large crowd. The noise abated. "It is a privilege for me to talk about Rosa Cooper today." Again the crowd went wild with applause and noise. "Now, now let's quiet down so I can give Rosa not only a certificate but this well deserved bonus. Mrs. Rosa Cooper, please come forward for your monetary award."

When Rosa got up to approach the lectern the shouts and whistles resumed. Mr. Gordon handed her the certificate and check. Rosa was about to walk back to her chair when Mr. Gordon said, "Wait, Rosa. I'm not finished yet. Come back over here."

Rosa's face was flushed with curiosity. "What? There's more?"

The crowd hushed in anticipation. Some took sips of coffee, some took the last bite of their dessert, and a few coughed. The crowd had no idea what was about to happen, and neither did Rosa Cooper. Only five people knew what was coming next.

"Rosa Cooper, you've just seen how much these men love and honor you and how much we value your service here at Pacific Spruce Corporation. But Rosa, I'll bet you didn't know that among this crowd is a gentleman who loves you even more than we do. Today we have a surprise for you beyond your wildest dreams."

Rosa's hand went to her mouth, and suspense hung in the air.

Mr. Gordon looked straight at Rosa and said, "I have the distinct pleasure of reuniting you with your long lost son!"

Ben rose and proudly advanced to the lectern. A big smile beamed from his face. Rosa was stunned, unable to move. Rosa seemed to know instinctively that the man approaching her was indeed her son. She began sobbing. Her arms opened wide and the two embraced. Cheers roared from the audience. People stood and clapped.

"We all wish you the best," Mr. Gordon said.

The ceremony closed with yet more applause. As the crowd was leaving the hall Rosa looked carefully at Ben. "I've looked so long for my son. Is it really you?"

"I've been looking for you too. I'd almost given up hope. Then I heard about you working here."

"Let me show you the kitchen, it's more private in there," Rosa said.

"I want to see where you work," Ben said. "And find out everything that's happened in your life."

As they walked from the hall Ben saw Eva in conversation with Mr. Gordon.

Chapter Twenty-five

"Would you like to take a tour of our plant?" Mr. Gordon asked Eva.

"Yes I would," Eva said. "I must warn you, I'm not an admirer of your operation."

"I've read your articles, and I've heard your father speak. Wouldn't you like to see the other side of the argument? Maybe you might change your mind."

"I don't see how I could, but I'm open to all points of view." Eva followed Mr. Gordon out of the cafeteria.

"This is where the lumber is sorted and stacked," Mr. Gordon said as he led Eva to the huge shed-like buildings beside the main sawmill. "This is the green chain—a belt that brings the cut lumber from the main mill. Men pull the wood off of them and stack it in these piles."

Eva followed Mr. Gordon into the building that housed the main sawmill operation. Giant vertical posts supported huge rafters that held up the thirty-foot-tall roof.

Mr. Gordon showed Eva the big saws that cut the incoming logs. "These specially designed carriages move the big logs into steam-powered saws. The saws slice the logs. Moving chains carry the resulting slabs of wood in various directions to be cut into dimensional lumber."

Large, debarked spruce logs lay waiting to be rolled onto the carriages. A log on one of the carriages had already passed through the steam saw once, leaving a long flat section where a slab of lumber had been sheared off. Eva noticed that the diameter of the log was considerably higher than she was tall. She looked out the windows and in the distance could see barren hillsides. Once green with conifers but now dull gray and lifeless. She felt sick. The entire sawmill operation was just a way to strip the land of elegant forests, unique to the world.

The voice of Mr. Gordon brought Eva back to reality. "Let me show you some of our other buildings." They walked out of the main sawmill and into the lumber yard. "That building off to your left is our planning mill. The other buildings are all necessary for preparing the lumber for market. Of course this is just a small part of the entire operation, but that's all we have time for today. Let's go back to the cafeteria."

"I'd like that," Eva said.

Chapter Twenty-six

Once in the kitchen Ben and Rosa sought out a private corner. Ben was able to observe his mother close up. Rosa was plump but with a robust vigor about her. Her blues eyes sparkled, and from the years of managing the big cafeteria she had a certain authority and confidence. She wore a spotlessly clean-full-length white dress covered with a white apron. She sat down at one of two chairs. She motioned to Ben to sit next to her.

"What a wonderful day—a day I'll never forget. Where do we start to get acquainted? I guess I can start by telling you that after I sent you off with my best friends, I moved into a home for smallpox victims. I really expected that I'd die soon. I can't explain it and neither could the doctor, but I got better. When I realized that I wasn't contagious anymore I went off in search of you. The friends I had relied on died in an accident. I learned that you had been shuttled off with other people. The frustrating part was I couldn't find out who they were. Nobody could help me and at last, out of money, I gave up and prayed you were safe. I decided to dedicate my life to the smallpox colony. After all, I had lost my husband, and then you. What more could I lose. I was depressed. I made life for the patients as comfortable as possible. Most of them passed away of course, and one was a relative of the owner here. Before she died she told Mr. Gordon about the care I had given her. One day he showed up and offered me this job. I worked a while longer at the colony, then took the job at this mill. After two weeks on the job I took over management of the cafeteria. I've been here ever since."

Ben told about his childhood, his growing up, his graduation from college, and the great opportunity working for the *Oregonian*. They confided deeper feelings as well. Ben told Rosa about his feelings of inadequacy and how he had been picked on his whole life because of his mole and small size. The jibes of his peers had left him with a lack of self-respect. He confided in her how he had hoped that this trip up the Coast would allow him to get a promotion, and that the new respect would allow him to conquer his fears. He also told her how he felt he was not good enough for his beautiful consort. He admitted to his mother that he was hopelessly in love with her.

"Maybe that's why we've finally bumped into each other," Rosa said.

"What do you mean?" Ben said.

"These feelings of inadequacy probably haunt you because you have no idea how brave your father was. He was a fearless man—kind and considerate, yet he'd stand up for values he felt were just. I have yet to meet another man quite like that."

Ben pulled his chair a little closer.

"Oh, yes, he was short like you. He had blazing blue eyes like you too. His strength was uncanny. He didn't have an ounce of fat on his bones, yet to look at him one would have thought he was a weakling. Honestly, I can't explain it, but every cell of his body bristled in strength. He could whip men three times his size. Bullies never dared challenge him. Could it be, Ben, that you have never tested your strength?"

"I don't honestly know. I've always run away

from bullies."

"That doesn't mean you're a weakling. Nobody wants to take a beating. But if you decide to stop and face the consequences you might discover your father's strength. It's in your blood, dear. You may have more of your father in you than you think."

Ben tensed up, hardly believing what he was hearing.

"Your father was a 'high climber.'"

"What's a high climber?" Ben asked.

"Why, the logging companies would call Frank Cooper to set up their spar trees at the companies' landings. The spar tree is the center of the logging operation, the tree used to pull the cut trees up the hill to the landing. He'd climb the tree with his saw and axe dangling on ropes from his hips, cutting and trimming branches as he climbed. He used cleated shoes and a belt around the tree trunk to help him climb. It was hard, dangerous work, and not many men were game for it. When he'd removed all the branches he'd saw off the top of the tree. When the top fell the tree would sway back and forth. Your father would ride it like a bull in a rodeo."

Rosa moved closer. "Then your father would do an amazing stunt. He'd climb on top of the spar tree and stand with his arms raised up. The men below would gasp, thinking he'd surely fall. I saw him do that twice. Why, your father was braver than any man I've ever met."

"What happened to him," Ben asked.

"One day there was an accident at the landing site—when the logs were being dragged in. One man was knocked unconscious when a tree sideswiped him. Another tree was rolling down toward the injured man at a tremendous speed. Your father was the only one to see the situation and try to help. He reached the downed logger and threw him over his shoulder. Then he started running for safety, but it was too late. The log crushed them both. But, your father died trying to save another. So you see, your father was not only fearless, he was also a hero."

Ben's eyes widened. "My God! I can't be any more proud of my father and mother than I am right now." For the first time in Ben's life he forgot about his mole, he forgot about having been called sissy, and he forgot about being everyone's punching bag. Plus, he forgot about having to get coffee for his editor. For the first time in his life he felt different, he felt whole. He finally had answers to the questions that had plagued him since childhood.

Ben hugged his mother. "I swear to you mother, I'll no longer be afraid. Learning about my father has helped me a lot. Maybe you're right; there is a reason why we met." They embraced again. Ben kissed his mother on the cheek and she reciprocated.

"Mother, I'd like to stay here and talk with you forever. This has been great meeting you."

"It's been wonderful, the best day of my life," Rosa said.

"Unfortunately the timing is bad," Ben said. "I have an assignment to complete for the newspaper. As soon as I'm done I'll be back to spend lots of time with you. At that time we'll get to know each other better. I'll write you often. But before I go, I'd like to introduce you to Eva." Ben and his mother went out the door of the kitchen and into the big cafeteria. Eva was still talking with the mill owner at a big table.

"Mr. Gordon, don't you see?" Eva was saying. "Once these virgin spruce and fir forests are destroyed they can't be replaced."

Mr. Gordon laughed, "New trees grow all the time."

"It's not the same as the old forest," Eva snapped. "You're the money and brains behind this operation. You need to stop cutting down precious old trees immediately!"

"Stop getting so upset. The forests will re-grow with time and look the same as it does now. My company provides jobs for the people in this area. Don't you see what we've created? I've just shown you the biggest mill in the world. We're paying for schools, roads, and other community projects. Your wild statements are completely inaccurate. You, my dear, are dead wrong."

"I'm right about this, Mr. Gordon!" Eva said heatedly. "I know I'm right!"

Mr. Gordon was about to pound his fist on the table when he caught sight of Rosa.

"Just one more word. Remember this!" Mr. Gordon whispered something in Eva's ear. Ben couldn't hear what the mill owner was saying. He saw Eva blush and break into tears. Mr. Gordon abruptly got up, forcing his chair back in such fury that it bounced off the neighboring table. He walked off in a huff.

"What's wrong, Eva?" Ben asked.

Tears flooded down her cheeks as she looked up at Ben and Rosa. She quickly straightened up in her chair and wiped away her tears. "I'm alright."

Ben put his arm around her shoulder trying to comfort her. "I don't like to see you crying."

"I'll be alright, honestly."

"I've brought someone special for you to meet," Ben said. "Eva, I want you to meet my mother."

Eva stood and shook Rosa's hand.

"Ben's been telling me about you," Rosa said. "He thinks you're the greatest."

Eva smiled.

"I've told mother that we have to leave soon," Ben added. "We need to reach Kernville before dark."

"It's a shame we have to go so soon," Eva said.

"I've got to prepare the evening snack, too," Rosa said. "As Ben said the timing for our get together is bad. Let's plan on meeting again soon when we all have more time."

"After we've completed our assignments we'll be back," Ben said. "You can count on that."

"Rosa, do you know of any interesting spots north of here?" Eva asked.

"You ought to stop at Bayocean's natatorium at Tillamook Bay. Take a few hours off, relax and swim at their pool. It's heated and actually has waves. That's something you could write about in your story."

"I'd like that," Eva said.

"What's the best road to take to get to Kernville?" Ben asked.

"Go back to Newport, then north through Otter Rock. After Otter Rock the road is dirt but since it's not raining you shouldn't have any problems."

Once back in the coupe Ben reached over, pulled Eva close, and kissed her. With his new-found self esteem he wasn't about to let this beautiful, sensitive woman out of his life. Ben knew he'd have to deal with Tom someday, but now he felt up to the challenge.

"Why were you crying in there?" Ben asked. "What did Mr. Gordon say?"

"He said if I write anymore articles maligning his coast logging operation he'd have my father removed from the OAC faculty and he'd denounce me as a slut." She burst into tears.

Without hesitation Ben threw open the car door. "Wait here!"

"Where are you going?" Eva asked.

"To give my mother another kiss," he said, and he was gone.

Ben rushed back into the cafeteria. He found Mr. Gordon at a desk in a small office adjoining the big cafeteria room. Mr. Gordon stood up with a grin. The grin didn't last long because Ben smashed his fist into it, knocking the man ruthlessly to the floor.

"Don't ever talk to Eva like that again!" Ben roared. He turned and walked through the big cafeteria and back to the waiting car.

Eva asked, "Was your mother happy that you'd come back to give her one more kiss?"

"Oh yes," Ben said. And he started the engine with his knuckles still aching.

"What all did you find out about your past from your mother?" Eva asked.

Ben explained what his mother had revealed to him about his heritage.

"I'm so glad you found her," Eva said. "Maybe now you'll believe what I've been saying, you're a courageous man, Ben."

Ben reddened at the praise, and quickly changed the subject.

"I'd like to go see that natatorium my mother talked about."

"Me too," Eva said. "But I can't help worrying about Tom. He's still out here somewhere. I wish he'd leave us alone."

"He's crazy, Eva. The only thing that will satisfy him is to have you in his power. I promise you I'll never let that happen."

Chapter Twenty-seven

Parked on a logging road that overlooked the big mill, Tom peered through his telescope. He saw the coupe parked in front of the cafeteria. That morning he had missed another opportunity to shoot Ben because of the lady riding with him. Shooting Ben with a witness like that around would have been foolhardy. Tom figured he'd simply have to wait for another opportunity.

Tom checked his watch. It was four thirty when he saw Ben and Eva drive away from the plant.

Once he had Eva back, he'd decided he'd head up to Washington and then drive into Canada. My God, he thought, I need to catch her soon. Time is running out. Tom drove slowly from his vantage point. His black sedan wove its way down the barren hillside like a shiny sexton black beetle clambering over the duff. Tom followed Ben's coupe at a safe distance. He followed them through Newport, and on a good road that paralleled the ocean's sandy beach. Just before reaching Otter Rock he lost sight of them.

Blakely Kidnapped

Chapter Twenty-eight

"At last we're back on a good road," Ben said. The coupe breezed along spewing gravel pellets in the air. It was as if they didn't have a care in the world. The coupe weaved in and out of forests, alongside cresting waves, and over headlands.

"Oh no," Eva said. "There's a bank of dark clouds behind us."

"I'm going to try and keep ahead of them," Ben said.

Just beyond Otter Rock the road suddenly turned to dirt. Ben knew it would be almost impassable once the rain hit. Ben tried to push the coupe as fast as it would go. They bounced and banged along in a race against the approaching storm.

"Look," Eva said. "It's pouring rain behind us." The sun darted in and out of clouds. To the east loomed thick lush forests, forests so dense that logging capitalists like Mr. Gordon probably hungered for first rights to the timber. The lumber in those forests would make him rich, Ben thought. He wondered what Eva was thinking as she gazed at the dense stand of tall conifers. Evening was approaching fast. Ben knew they would have to camp soon.

"Can we camp here tonight?" Eva asked and pointed to an opening.

"Sure." Ben wondered why she had picked this spot. The opening was a wide deer path that veered off into the forest. The car almost sank in the soft forest soil. Young hemlocks sprouted from a mammoth decaying Douglas fir. Salal, ferns, huckleberries, and Oregon grape scratched against his car.

It seemed to Ben as if they had been swallowed by the vegetation. A mist hovered over the ground. Ben had never been in an ancient forest before at least none like this. The storm that had followed them drifted east.

"We shouldn't go any farther," Eva said. "Let's park next to that big cedar."

Ben parked the car. He knew he'd have to back out the same way they came in. He prayed it wouldn't rain overnight.

When the motor was turned off Eva said, "Listen to the silence, Ben. Isn't it wonderful? It's almost unearthly. Have you ever been in a primeval forest like this?"

"No," Ben said. "It's humbling. It sounds like these old trees are talking to us in whispers."

"Maybe they're asking us to save them," Eva said.

"Well, if Mr. Gordon has his way, I can understand why they're scared."

They got out of the car and set their tent up on the moss-covered ground. The fragrance of the cedar boughs drifted by. Ancient Douglas firs and Sitka spruce trees dominated the woods, leaving little room for other trees. Decaying giant trees lay haphazardly across the terrain. The giant pillars and ever changing shades of green filled Ben's senses.

"You almost squashed that slug," Eva scolded. "Be careful where you walk."

Ben picked up the ten inch long slug and placed it in a shady spot. A red three inch salamander, with a yellow stripe on its back, scooted out of Ben's way. Ben saw a little tailed frog. He watched it leap into the brush. A twenty foot snag jutted up in front of him. An enormous pileated woodpecker with a bright red crest hammered away on the snag's bark.

They put down their ground blankets near the tent's door so they could peer up through the tall trees. Daylight still lingered as they lay on their backs and became more aware of their surroundings. Ben and Eva stared toward the heavens. The sky was barely visible through the dense canopy.

"See how the fir trees tower above the rest," Eva said.

"I'd bet they're two hundred feet high," Ben said.

"They must be over four hundred years old," Eva said. "Why is the preservation of the redwood forests more important than the preservation of the Oregon Coast Range forest? If there is a redwood society trying to preserve those forests, why can't we have a society here in Oregon that would buy up land to protect ours?"

"Looking at these trees it's hard not to agree with you. Maybe Jess was right when he told me I'd learn a lot on this trip. Maybe I've been wrong, trying to defend the lumber industry. They'll stand up for themselves. Maybe you're right about saving these ancient forests. Why have I been so stubborn?"

"Sometimes it's hard to stand up for what's right when everyone else thinks differently," Eva said. "Until now, you haven't seen the forest yourself."

"Thanks to you and your father, I may be changing my mind. You're like a rose in a sea of thistles, Eva. I really admire your bravery. I wonder what this land will be like if these forests are chopped down?

"I think it's all about money," Eva said.

"If that's true, then I've certainly been backing the wrong side." Ben noticed a slight grin forming on Eva's lips.

"Why else would we destroy these marvelous places? It's beautiful here."

"It's more then that," Ben said. "It's spiritual."

"We can help convince people of that, Ben." Eva

said. "We have the power of the pen. We should use it before it's too late."

Shadows were blurring into the dark of night. The air was pungent with the smell of decaying forest, fresh and exuberant. Ben took a deep breadth.

"This is paradise," Eva said.

"It's as close to paradise as I've ever been," Ben said. Both were still peering upwards when Ben's arm found its place under Eva's head. His heart began to beat fast. Eva turned toward him. He turned too and they embraced, holding each other close. Ben felt Eva's soft lips in a long rapturous kiss. When it ended they both fell back again, looking skyward.

"Do you see it?"

"The first star out, yes I do." Ben felt as if he were zooming above the tips of the trees, above the earth's atmosphere, and up to the stars. He looked down on the two prone shapes staring up from the dense forest. It seemed like his life now had a purpose. Before, he had just functioned. He had done what he was told to do. From now on he and Eva would be the voice of the Oregon Coast forest. He loved Eva and knew she loved him. With this new sense of oneness, his mind settled back to earth. He could hear Eva's breathing, and he felt united with her.

"I plan to stand up for myself, for you, and for this wonderful ancient place," Ben said. He felt Eva's hand grip his tightly. She wiggled closer.

"If we could only get Tom off our trail," Ben whispered.

"We will," Eva said.

Ben looked at Eva in the fading light. She was enchanting, beautiful, and inviting. The giant trees rustled in the wind, and from the branches Ben heard the hoot of an owl. He got up on one elbow and looked into Eva's eyes. For a moment they stared spellbound, as if they were the only people in the world. Then their lips touched. They held the kiss for a long while before parting. Ben was exhilarated as he saw the sparkle in Eva's eyes. The rest of that night they slept little.

The trip up Oregon's Coast had changed Ben's future in many ways. He had found his mother, he had found his courage, he had found Eva, and now, he found his manhood.

Chapter Twenty-nine

Tom hadn't had any trouble keeping them in sight from Toledo to Otter Rock because the road was in good shape. It was smooth gravel. In fact, Tom got so close one time he feared they could have spotted him. He noticed the dark clouds rapidly approaching from the west. At a vantage point just past Otter Rock, where the road became dirt and poorly graded, he saw the coupe bumping along at a furious pace. That's when the rain began to fall. Lightly at first, then in sheets that pounded off his hood and through his broken window. It was coming down at gale force, slashing against his car at a thirty-five degree angle. The rain was so thick he could hardly see the muddy road ahead. His tires began spinning in the mud. Damn it, it's like grease out there, he thought.

He stopped the car and stepped out into the pouring rain. He climbed into the back of the car to get his tire chains. Once he had them, he went to the back wheels and began putting the chains on. His hat dripped water on his hands, and his clothing soaked up the rain. Hunching over the tire he eventually had one wrapped. The second one was easier. By the time he was able to return to the driver's seat, water dripped from every part of his body.

He shifted into first gear and slowly drove forward. Soon his chained wheels began to spin. I've got to get through this mud, he thought. But he was going nowhere. His car was stuck in the mud up to its hubcaps.

He opened his car door, got out in the storm, and slammed it shut. Water sprayed against him. He looked at his rear wheels and almost cried. He was so frustrated that he wished he could go back home, but there was no home to go back to. Then he saw a car with its head lamps barely visible approaching him. The car drove right up to where he was stuck. Four men got out.

"Need help, mister?" one man asked.

"Please, I need to get moving."

"Come on, guys. Let's see if we can get this car out."

Three hours later they were all still working. "This is useless," one of the men said.

"The weather is letting up," another said.

"We'll just have to wait it out," the driver said. "By morning we should be able to get going again. Let's get some rest."

"You have to help me," Tom said.

"In the morning," the driver said gruffly.

Damn those lazy bastards, Tom thought.

Exhausted, he climbed into the backseat. There he took on a helpless fetal position. Tom was shivering. He pulled his wet coat over his shoulders and dropped off into a convulsive sleep.

Chapter Thirty

Ben opened his eyes and heard the faint breathing of Eva. She was sound asleep. Shafts of sunlight filtered through the giant pillars of tree trunks. A small fir cone bounced to the ground. Wrens and chickadees sang as they flitted through the trees. A Steller's jay scolded from above.

Ben saw Eva's eyes open. "Good morning."

"Can we stay here forever?" Eva whispered.

"No," Ben said regretfully. "It's about noon. We have to get going. I'm hoping that going to Bayocean will throw Tom off our trail—if he's still behind us. We'll rent a cabin and get a good night sleep and swim before continuing on."

"All right," Eva said.

Something crashed about in the shrubbery next to them. An animal grunted.

"What's that?" Eva asked, frightened silly.

Ben sat up. "Whoa!"

A black bear burst from the bushes and almost ran over them in his effort to scramble away. It loped off into the forest, smashing small hemlocks and crashing through the salal. Then it stopped at the base of a giant fir.

"He's looking back this way," Ben said.

Eva put the blanket over her head.

"There he goes! He's running away. He must be afraid of us."

"Thank goodness," Eva said from under the covers. They hurriedly got up and started folding their bedding.

Then they folded the tent and stowed it next to the camera gear in the rear of the car. When they had finished packing things away, Ben noticed that Eva was calmer.

"I need you to decide which hat I should wear. The red one or the blue one," Eva said. She posed with her head tilted to one side, then the other, exhibiting each hat with a silly smile on her face.

"I like the red hat best. It matches the color of that robin's breast," Ben said. They looked at the robin and laughed as it hopped around under the cedar tree parading its beautiful red breast.

"Okay, then it's red," Eva said.

Ben had enjoyed the closeness that this isolated spot had fostered between them. Time was going much too fast. It was already Monday. He wanted to spend two more nights here with Eva. But he had an article to write and he worried that Tom might catch up. They finished packing and got into the coupe.

Ben looked over at Eva. "Last night was the best time I've had in my entire life."

"Mine too," Eva said. Ben squeezed Eva's hand. Then he shifted the car into reverse and backed up on the same track they had followed the night before. Soon they were breezing along on the Roosevelt Highway.

Once on the highway they held hands as the scenery flew by. Soon they reached the Siletz River and boarded a ferry. North of Kernville the highway was an unexpected delight–it was fine gravel. They zoomed along, passing through the towns of Delake, Neskowin, Hebo, and Hemlock. Ben drove the 35-mile-an-hour speed limit, swirling dust up behind them. Soon they were on the southern edge of Tillamook. Dairy farms stretched for miles. They stopped at the first gas station in town. The attendant greeted them with a broad smile.

"Fill it up," Ben said. The attendant removed the gas hose and stuck the nozzle into the gas tank.

Ben stuck his head out the window. "We've heard a lot about the resort out on the spit, Bayocean. Can you tell us how to get there?"

"You're in luck," the gas attendant said. "Men have been working on the road that goes out there, but yesterday they were pulled off the job to work on the Roosevelt Highway south of Kernville. I tried out the road yesterday and was able to drive all the way to Bayocean. Don't get me wrong. There's still a lot of work to be done before it's finished. But if you really want to get out there, and you're careful, it's passable. Just follow the shore of Tillamook Bay. It will take you directly to the spit."

"Thanks," Ben said, paying the man. As they drove from the station Ben could feel the warmth of Eva's hand as their grasp was reunited. They turned off the highway on the bay road heading west. The road was rough in many places, with soft sand, vacated work zones, and small fordable streams. Some of the sandy spots were rocked for easy passage. Other places their wheels sank and Ben feared they might get stuck. Driving was slow and tedious but eventually they were able to make it out to the spit of land that separated the bay from the ocean.

Once there, Ben delighted in the paved roads, which made driving easy in the little resort town. They drove Bay Boulevard to the center of town.

Eva spotted a group of small cabins. "Let's see if we can rent one of those."

At the office Ben registered them as man and wife. The clerk informed them that they would be unable to use the telephone. The lines had been temporarily taken down due to the road construction.

"We won't need a phone," Ben said.

"Here's your key. If you need anything just come back to the office."

"Eva and Ben inspected the one-room cabin. After bringing in their gear from the car they freshened up and arranged the room to the way they wanted it. Then hand in hand they walked out of the cabin on a path toward the ocean. They climbed up a sand bank overlooking the Pacific Ocean. The huge natatorium stood surprisingly close to the crashing waves on the beach.

Ben looked out at the panoramic view, thinking how much his relationship with Eva had grown in a such short time. "Eva, this past week has been the best week of my life. Until now I haven't been able to express my love, I guess because I didn't have the confidence. But my mother opened my eyes. Now that I know my heritage, I'm not afraid to tell you how I feel."

Eva gripped his hand tighter.

Ben looked into Eva's eyes. "I've grown to love you, Eva. I won't waste another second of my life without asking, will you marry me?"

"Oh, yes!" came the quick response. "Yes, yes, yes!" They embraced and held a long kiss.

As they kissed the waves crashed against the sand in a rhythmic cadence, the wind whipped at their clothing, and seagulls soared overheard.

Chapter Thirty-one

Ben's eyes opened and his lips parted from Eva's. Once again he could hear the roar of the ocean and feel the wind. He had never been so happy. He led the way back to the cabin and waited outside as Eva put on her swimming suit. Ben hugged her when she came back out though the door. Then it was Eva's turn to wait. From the cabin they walked hand in hand, following signs to the natatorium. The path led up to a sandy ridge covered with grass and six foot brushes. On the other side they walked down to the crashing waves and then south towards the natatorium.

The sea washed over their feet, swirling cold water around their ankles. Looming ahead was the two-story enclosed swimming pool. Ben held open the big entry doors for Eva. Inside was the biggest swimming pool Ben had ever beheld. Filled with ocean water, it was heated by a gigantic fireplace at the far end of the pool. Above them was the second story balcony where people stood gawking down at the swimmers below. Huge open beams with some of the largest finished lumber Ben had ever seen stretched the width of the building's ceiling. He would have to tell his readers about this building.

They laid their towels at the pool's edge and Eva set down her red hat. Then they entered the warm water at the shallow end and waded toward the center of the pool. They splashed water on each other and chased each other around like a couple of kids. Other swimmers had to get out of their way. People in the balconies laughed and pointed. They were just getting used to the water when Eva doubled over in pain.

"What's wrong?" Ben asked, concerned.

"Cramps," Eva whispered. "Sometimes I get cramps so bad that I have to lie down for a while. You stay here and swim. I'm going back to our cabin and rest awhile. Give me about an hour and then come back. I should be ready for dinner by then."

"I can't let you go back to the cabin alone," Ben said. "I wouldn't enjoy it here with out you, anyway."

"I need some time. I swear I'll be okay," Eva said."

"No," Ben said sternly. He followed her out of the pool to the towels. They dried themselves off and put on their robes. Ben watched as Eva adjusted her pretty felt hat on her wet head. She tried to smile, but then grimaced. Ben sensed her pain and led her outside through the big double doors.

Chapter Thirty-two

It was noon when sunlight through the car windows woke Tom, interrupting his snoring. He opened his eyes cautiously. Let me sleep! he thought. He kicked off his soggy coat. Sitting up, he yawned deeply. His beard was thick stubble. He reeked like a dog that had never been bathed. He opened the car door, got out, and stretched. The car with the four men was gone. "Those bastards," he muttered. He tested the ground with his boot heel. It was hard enough to drive on, he thought. He brushed back his thick hair with his hand. Then he got back in his sedan. The car started easily. He pushed in the clutch and shifted into reverse. He pushed gently down on the gas, then shifted into first gear, and then reverse, working his car backward and forward until he was free from the mud. Once out, he drove north towards the Siletz River.

Maybe things will go better today, he thought. His damp clothes still made him shiver, but the warmth of the sun was helping. The day was so clear he could see for miles. The Ford bumped and banged along on the dirt road for fourteen miles until at last he could see the ferry landing and the craft that would take him across the Siletz River and into the community of Kernville.

The ferry brought two cars to the landing. The barge slowly bumped against pilings and settled in place right in front of Tom. With little fanfare the cars on the ferry rolled off and Tom's car jostled to get on. Once aboard he paid the thirty-five cent fare and waited as the ferry steamed off into the current.

The ferry captain complained to Tom all the way across. "I'll be out of a job once that dang bridge is built. It's upriver from here. I don't know what I'll do. It's a beautiful steel bridge, but a lot of good that does me. I've two children and a wife to provide for. I just don't know what I'll do. It's frustrating."

Tom was frustrated too, but he wasn't listening to the captain. Tom's mind was on Eva. He could hardly wait to get off the ferry. As soon as he drove ashore his car sailed along on the good road until he felt the nagging thump of a flat tire. He repaired it himself, but it took half an hour. Back on the road, it wasn't long before he experienced a second flat. Now he was out of spare tires. He had to wait two hours for a car to stop so he could barrow a spare. All this took precious time.

Tom didn't reach Tillamook until six p.m. He stopped at the first gas station he came to. While the attendant was fueling his car Tom asked him if he had seen a coupe with a man and woman. The attendant told Tom about Ben and Eva.

"I'm trying to catch up with them," Tom said. "They're friends of mine. How do I get to Bayocean?"

"Believe me, that road is plenty rough—but it's passable. It's the only road out there. Just follow the shoreline of Tillamook bay." Tom paid the man and headed for Bayocean.

Tom took his time on the deserted road that led out to the spit, hoping he would see the coupe. This would be a good spot for an ambush, he reasoned. Even if he didn't see their car he knew that all this chasing would soon be over. The way Tom saw it, they were trapped on a spit of land. Trapped like coons up a tree. He was certain that Eva would be in his possession soon. He had it all worked out. If she resisted coming with him, he'd use the morphine. He looked forward to finally getting his Eva back.

It was almost dark when he arrived in Bayocean. He slowly drove into town on Bay Boulevard. He turned off at the sign pointing to the natatorium, figuring that they might well head there. He found a parking spot behind some windswept shrubbery. Tom picked up his revolver and checked to make sure it was loaded. Then he carefully placed the gun inside his shirt and tucked it under his belt. He squirmed as the cold metal touched his skin. Tom got out of the car and walked towards the beach. He followed a sandy path that led up through the thick bushes to the crest of the hill. Once at the top he could see the natatorium to his left. Coming out from the double doors were Ben and Eva.

Tom couldn't believe his eyes. There they were walking towards him. He knew they would have to come up his path. No one was around. Tom hid in the bushes.

He saw them start to climb up the path. I'm in luck, for once I'm in luck! He thought. His heart began to pound. Soon Eva would be his. He heard them scrape through the bushes only a few feet away. Tom pulled the gun from his belt and held it by the barrel. Ben was nearest as they approached. Tom jumped out and smashed the butt of his gun on Ben's head. Ben let out a short groan and hit the sand hard, senseless.

"Ben!" Eva cried. "What have you done?" Then Tom smashed his left fist into her temple. She toppled onto the sand unconscious. Tom quickly pulled Eva and Ben out of sight into the bushes. He checked them— they were breathing, but out cold. Tom peered out through the bushes, still no one around. Then he aimed the pistol at Ben's head. Oh, how he wanted to pull the trigger but feared the noise would bring people.

Suddenly two children, young boys, came running

up the path. They were racing for the natatorium. They were dressed in swimming suits and held towels in their hands.

Tom put the gun back in his belt. Then he picked Eva up in his arms and carried her toward his car. Her head hung limply. He laid her on the backseat, tied her hands behind her, and tied her feet. He got out his handkerchief and cleaned around her mouth. Then he kissed her, and then he kissed her again hard. "I have you back my Eva, I have you back!" He withdrew from the backseat like a snake from a hole, and took the driver's seat. Overhead a few stars began appearing.

On Bay Boulevard, his head lamps illuminated the road. A full moon lit the sky. Tom's car weaved a bit until it reached the road under construction that led into Tillamook. Tom reeled with a new sensation that jumped from high elation to depression. Eva was his until death. If one of them died so would the other, he thought. Turning his head to the backseat he said, "Eva, we better hurry. We don't have much time before the police discover what's happened." He hoped it would take a long time for Ben to regain consciousness. Tom knew he had hit him awfully hard. Hell, he might even be dead, Tom thought, smiling.

The sedan squished along on sand and rocks. Off in the distance, Tom could hear the roar of the ocean as the tide was ebbing. He tried to skirt a dampened area but sank into the soft sand. His tires spun wildly and lost traction.

"Another soggy road," he said. "It won't be long, Eva. I'll get us out of this. I'm an expert at getting out of mud." He got out his shovel and started digging around the back tires. When he had cleared the sand away, he went in search of some driftwood and brush to place under them. After about two hours he finally got back in the car and started the engine. Then he shifted into low gear. He pushed down on the throttle slowly nudging the car forward and out of the sand. Once again he was free and on his way to Tillamook, with Eva's bound body lying unconscious on the sedan's backseat.

Chapter Thirty-three

When Ben first opened his eyes everything was a blur. He felt dizzy and nauseous. His head ached. He gently touched the bloody bump on his heard. He immediately flinched in pain and closed his eyes. He got up on his knees and rested with his hands on the ground. He knew he had to get moving, and fast. So he stood up, but then he blacked out again and fell over into the bushes. The stiff branches poked and cut his arms. After five minutes he awoke again. This time he waited for his eyes to focus. He got up slowly. Ben staggered through the grassy area, nearly falling again. Then he saw Eva's red hat, almost hidden in the grass. He stooped to pick it up, but grew dizzy and had to stay crouched until his head cleared. Finally he began walking back to the cabin.

By the time he reached the cabin's front door he had recovered enough to start planning his next move. Ben went inside, dressed hurriedly, and gathered their belongings. He knew Tom had kidnapped Eva. I'll call and alert the police first, Ben thought. But then he remembered the clerk informing them that the telephone lines were down. So, his only alternative was to follow Tom himself. He went outside to his coupe. He threw his and Eva's clothes on the passenger seat. Then he started the car. Soon he was speeding along on the paved spit towards the bay access road.

Ben turned from the spit to the sandy construction road. About a mile up the road he saw Tom's car. Ben nearly shouted "They're stuck in the mud!" But just then he saw Tom's car move forward, freed from the sand. Ben hoped he could keep up. In his haste, Ben drove through the same soft sand and he too became mired down. "Oh shit!" Ben threw his car door open and jumped out. For a moment his head throbbed so badly he almost blacked out again. Crawling back in the car he got his shovel. Because of his aching head, everything he did seemed in slow motion. He looked up and saw Tom's car disappearing toward Tillamook. After Ben had dug around his tires he spotted the wood and shrubs Tom had gathered. Ben put them under his tires.

Ben slowly drove out of the hole. A few feet away from the sandy area his tire went flat. "My God!" he shouted. He spent the next hour replacing the flat tire with his spare. When finished he once again sped along the construction road with his head lamps ablaze. The lights jumped wildly in the dark from one obstruction to the next. As he skirted around them he could see he was advancing towards the lights of Tillamook.

When he reached the Roosevelt Highway, in town, he had to make a decision. Which way had Tom gone? Ben wondered. If Tom went south towards Newport the authorities would surely stop him. If he went north towards Astoria he might be able to escape into Washington. That must be the direction he had taken. So Ben turned left and drove through Tillamook with a full moon lighting his way. When he reached Bay City the road turned from good gravel to a combination of barely graded dirt, and wood planks. Jolting up and down on the plank road made Ben's head ache.

Chapter Thirty-four

It was late Monday evening when Tom's car banged over the plank road between Wheeler and Mohler. The thumping noise and bouncing ride roused Eva. She began screaming, wriggling and kicking with all her strength to get free.

"Shut up!" Tom snarled.

Eva shouted even louder.

"Okay you asked for it." Tom stopped the car. "I didn't want to do this," he said, getting the bottle of morphine from the front seat. He opened the back door and slapped Eva hard. Then he lifted her head by the hair and pried open her mouth. He managed to pour some morphine in. She gagged and choked, but swallowed some of it. The rest she spat in his face. He butted his forehead against hers, momentarily shocking her. That allowed Tom to pour more morphine in her mouth. She couldn't help gulping it down. Tom held her down and tried to kiss her. Eva bit him. Tom jerked his head back. He slapped her so hard she fainted.

When Tom let go of Eva he noticed blood dripping onto Eva's face. His chin was dripping where Eva had bitten him. He used his handkerchief to stop the bleeding. Then he covered Eva with a blanket and got back in the driver's seat. All this took precious time. He knew that Ben and possibly the authorities weren't far behind.

Tom was relieved when he finally got back on a good dirt road. I hate those plank roads, he thought.

After driving a while he reached a Y in the road. One way led to the ocean beach and Hug Point, the old established route. The other led to the new highway, but it was under construction. A sign indicated the new highway was closed. Tom took the road to Hug Point.

Chapter Thirty-five

As the coupe wobbled over the plank road, Ben's head felt like an ice cream churn, continually being cranked. It felt like his head was going to explode. His teeth chattered as the car bounced from one plank to the next. At last he returned to a dirt surface. The plank road had been the worst he'd ever driven on. Ben plodded along through the towns of Garibaldi, Rockaway, and Brighton. His mind cleared. Even with the help of the full moon, there was still no sight of Tom's sedan.

After the town of Mohler, he saw the Y in the road, and the highway construction site. Construction equipment lay along the road like sleeping dinosaurs. The machinery effectively blocked passage along that route. A sign pointed to Hug Point and Cannon Beach to the left. One thing Ben did know about the highway was that once he reached Seaside, just north of Cannon Beach, there would be good roads right into Astoria. He took the road that led to Hug Point. Soon he was driving on the beach, whizzing along at forty miles an hour on the hard sand. Oh, what a relief to be driving on this beach. It was smoother than a concrete highway, he thought.

The moon reflected off the wet sand of the receding tide, lighting up the beach ahead. He pushed the coupe to its fastest speeds. Mile after mile, he didn't even feel a bump. Then he had to slow down for a headland jutting out in the sand. Just as he rounded the obstruction, Hug Point came into view. Tom's tail lights were just vanishing around a sharp curve on the rocky road. Ben felt a surge of relief. He had made the right decision to turn north.

He drove gingerly over the sand to Hug Point, where his tires found traction on rock. To his right was a cliff. To his left was the sea. He slowly approached the sharp curve he had seen Tom's car disappear behind. Cautiously he drove around it.

Suddenly Ben saw a burst of red flame. There was a loud blast and the sound of the bullet ricocheting off rocks near his windshield. He quickly shifted into reverse and began backing up around the bend to safety. Two more shots rang out. Ben parked the car and quickly got out to see if he could spot Tom's car. He peered around the corner. To his horror the sedan's tail lights were backing up towards him.

Ben raced back to his auto and backed off Hug Point onto the sand. He scooted behind a headland in reverse, like a crab under a rock. He turned out his lights. Then he got out to see if Tom would follow.

Tom's car stopped at Hug Point, like a shark waiting in the shadows to attack its prey. Ben watched, holding his breath, it seemed forever. Then he let out a sigh of relief: Tom's car had begun bouncing over the rocky road headed north.

That was close, Ben thought.

Chapter Thirty-six

That coward, Tom thought. Maybe I hit him. That'll slow him down. The roles are now reversed, Ben Cooper. Now you have to chase me! How do you like it!

Tom shifted into first gear and drove slowly north over the cobblestone surface. After getting off the Hug Point road he eventually came into the town of Cannon Beach. From there the road was vastly improved. He made good time as he drove to the outskirts of Astoria. He saw the drawbridge being lifted as he drove up on the Young's Bay Bridge. Tom saw two cars lined up ahead of him. Chugging slowly, a big steamer going out to sea approached the bridge. It seemed hours before the steamer passed through the raised portions of road. By that time many cars had lined up behind him. They must be employees of nearby fish canning companies, Tom thought. Once the steamer had passed, the two sections of raised road lowered back down and realigned. Tom followed the traffic off the north side of the bridge. Then he turned east and drove along the banks of Young's Bay. About half a mile away from the bridge he stopped at a small turnout and looked back at the bridge to watch for Ben's car.

Chapter Thirty-seven

Ben got back in his car and carefully drove to Hug Point. He got out of his auto and walked to the sharp curve. He peered cautiously around the rocks. He could see the head-lights from Tom's car disappearing to the north. Ben quickly returned to his car and followed. When he reached Cannon Beach he stopped at a farmhouse. A light glowed on the front porch. He walked up the steps and knocked on the door. "Please let someone be home," Ben whispered.

It seemed an eternity before a woman's voice asked. "Who is it?"

"My name is Ben Cooper. I need to use your phone if you have one. It's an emergency."

"Ah… I don't know," the woman said. "My husband told me not to let anyone in."

"I'm a reporter from the *Oregonian*. I need to use your phone to call the police in Astoria. A life depends on it. Please, I beg you. Let me use your phone."

Ben heard the lock being undone. A heavy-set woman in a bright blue bathrobe opened the door. Her stiff hair reminded Ben of a dried mop.

"Over there," she said; pointing to the wall near the entry into the kitchen. "Wow," she added. "That's a nasty bump on your head."

Ben ignored her and hurried to the phone in the dimly lit room. He lifted the earpiece and heard a girl and man talking. Surprised, he hung the earpiece back up.

"It's an eight-party line," the farmwife explained.

"That's probably my neighbors Betty Jo and Hank. They talk all night sometimes."

"Can you do something?" Ben asked. "Anything?"

Mrs. Brown took the phone.

"Betty Jo, I need to use the phone. It's an emergency. Please hang up."

When the line was clear Ben tried again. "Please connect me to the Astoria police department. It's an emergency," Ben told the operator. He heard the phone ring at the other end of the line. A woman's voice answered.

"Astoria police station."

"This is Ben Cooper, a reporter for the *Oregonian*. There's a man headed for your area in a Ford sedan. He's kidnapped my fiancée. He's threatening to kill her. He almost killed me. You have to stop him."

"Who did you say he's kidnapped?" the woman asked.

"Eva Barton. She's a journalist too."

"And what is the name of the man we're supposed to stop?"

"His name is Tom Bigalow. He's been stalking Eva for over a week. A few hours ago he took her against her will. You have to find them."

"We'll definitely be on the lookout. There's a statewide warrant out for Bigalow's arrest. You say he's headed for Astoria?"

"Yes, he should be arriving there soon. Eva may need medical help, so you should have an ambulance with staff ready to treat her."

"Yes, we'll be ready. I only have one officer on duty at this time but the first shift comes in soon and they'll be alerted to what's happening."

"Thanks," Ben said, and hung the earpiece back in its cradle. Ben quickly thanked the farm wife as he headed out the door for his car. He heard the door lock behind him.

He drove like a racer on a speedway to the outskirts of Astoria. There was a long line of cars waiting at Young's Bay Bridge. The drawbridge was just lowering the two bridge segments into position. Once the road was back in position the cars would be able to drive through. He saw Tom's Ford near the front of the line. Ben got out thinking he might run up and catch Tom. But then he saw Tom's car move forward, following two other cars over the bridge. So Ben hurried back to his coupe. From behind the steering wheel he saw Tom's car as it turned east. He tried to keep an eye on both the traffic ahead of him and Tom's car. Then the traffic on the bridge came to a complete stop.

"Hey!" Ben complained. A policeman had just arrived and was inspecting each car. Ben had to wait, but kept a watch on Tom's car. He saw it stop for a while on the edge of the road as if Tom couldn't decide which way to go. Then Tom drove slowly up the hill and away from the bay.

Blakely   Kidnapped

Chapter Thirty-eight

The rising sun splashed a red glow on the eastern horizon. Tom looked back at the bridge. He noticed a police car drive up to it. A policeman got out and began stopping vehicles as they came off the bridge.

"My God," Tom said. "They're looking for me." For the first time since he left Corvallis he became truly alarmed. He pushed his hat back. Confusion and fear were setting in. Where to now, he thought? He drove up the hill on Seventh Street, hoping to cut through a residential area of Astoria. Once through town he could drive east along the Columbia River towards The Dalles. He figured the ferry that crossed from Astoria to Washington would also be watched by the police, but he might have better luck in The Dalles. Tom felt hurried and began to panic.

He came to a level spot on the road. The road divided, with one fork going steeply up the hill and the other continuing on into Astoria. The road going up the hill was blocked by movable wooden barriers. A sign read *Construction site. No Trespassing.* Maybe I can hide up there, Tom thought. They'll never think to look for me on that road. He got out of his car and moved the barriers to one side. Then he drove between them and stopped. He put the barriers back in place. With his foot he quickly shoved dirt over the tire tracks, trying to cover them. Then he drove up the winding road.

As Tom rounded the corner of Coxcomb Hill he saw a circular column of concrete towering above him.

It must be over a hundred feet tall, he thought. As he slowly drove around the column he noticed pieces of concrete, boards and debris strewn all over the place. He stopped the car, reached over to the passenger seat and picked up his revolver and stuck it in his belt. Tom got out of the car and tilted his head back, looking up at the column. Encircling the pillar just under the crown was wood scaffolding covered with canvas. The scaffolding hugged the concrete like a speared donut. The canvas twisted in the morning wind and banged against the sides of the column.

There was a moan from the back seat. Tom got the vial of morphine from the front seat. Then he opened the back door. Eva, let out another low moan, only to sink back into unconsciousness. Figuring she was unable to wake, he closed the door. Just then a gust of wind sent his hat sailing off into the air. It landed near the column entrance door. A piece of concrete propped open the door to the column. Tom peered up the inside the dark shaft. A staircase spun upwards. Tom felt frustrated, alone, and weary, as if time was running out on him. He threw the bottle of morphine against the inner concrete wall. It broke and crashed to the floor. He stomped on his hat and then kicked it. He felt trapped.

He returned to his car and opened the back door. Tom pulled Eva out of the car. He carried her, in his arms to the opened door of the column.

He took a deep breath and began the climb, limping up the staircase. His steps echoed off the concrete walls. He paused at each landing to catch his breath, readjusting his hold on Eva. When he reached the top landing he found the door leading to the balcony wedged open. He carried Eva outside and onto the ledge that overlooked the town of Astoria, the Columbia River, Young's Bay and the Pacific Ocean.

Chapter Thirty-nine

Finally it was Ben's turn to be checked by the policeman.

"What's your name sir?" Officer Stout asked.

"I'm Ben Cooper!" Ben exclaimed. "I'm the one who reported to your station that Tom Bigalow was coming to town. Tom's car just went up that hill over there. We have to get after him right away."

"That's Seventh Street," Officer Stout said. "I'll get my patrol car and you can follow me. Okay?"

Ben nodded, and the officer ran to get his car. Ben followed the officer as he drove up the hill. The officer stopped at the "No trespassing" sign, got out, and inspected the road. He quickly noticed the poor attempt to hide the car tracks. He motioned to Ben and pointed up the hill. The officer pulled the barriers from the middle of the road and quickly returned to his vehicle. Ben followed as they drove up the winding gravel road to the summit. The officer slowed down as he approached the open area beneath the column. Ben saw him park next to Tom's car. Ben parked next to the officer's vehicle.

Blakely   Kidnapped

Chapter Forty

One hundred feet below him, Tom saw the police car park next to his. He also saw Ben's coupe arrive. At the edge of the balcony was a ladder that led down onto the scaffolding. The wind banged the wood structure against the concrete so hard that the ladder came loose and fell to one side. Bits of the canvas covering flew off. Suddenly Tom had an idea. He laid Eva down, then he leaned over the rail and pulled the ladder back into position. He placed Eva over his shoulder. With the wind shaking the scaffolding from side to side he descended the swaying ladder and stepped onto the dangling wood platform. Then he put Eva down and grasped the ropes that controlled the pulleys. Tom lowered the circular scaffolding about twenty feet. He then locked the ropes in place, suspending the scaffolding seventy-five feet in the air.

Eva moaned. Tom shoved her farther under the canvas, hiding her from view. Then he returned to the wooden rail to watch what was happening below. He took out his gun, ready to defend Eva and himself. He saw the officer and Ben looking up.

Chapter Forty-one

Officer Stout and Ben both got out of their cars at the same time. They tilted their heads up.

"There's Tom," Ben said. "He's yelling something to us. Quick, get behind the cars." They scrambled for cover as two shots smacked the ground.

"I'm going up," Ben said. "Call for reinforcements and get that ambulance up here."

"Yes sir," Stout said.

When Ben saw Tom vanish under the canvas he knew Tom couldn't see the ground. Ben took the opportunity to make a rush to the column door and disappear inside. He climbed the staircase, bounding up the steps two at a time. His head was throbbing fiercely, but he continued anyway. When he neared the top he slowed, gasping for air. Once his breathing was under control he crept silently to the top landing. Ben peered out through the door. Clouds hovered on the western horizon. The sun had crested the mountains in the east. The landing outside the door extended about four feet and was bounded by a four-foot fence of horizontal boards held in place with vertical posts. He crept out onto the concrete landing and then peeked over the side. He couldn't hear anything but the wind blowing the platform against the concrete. He couldn't tell exactly where Tom and Eva were inside the canvas covered scaffolding. He crawled around to the east side. Shielding his eyes with his hand, he looked over the edge. It suddenly dawned on him why he had never been afraid of heights. His father had worked in the treetops. He remembered his mother saying how excited his father would get about his job. He was fearless, his mother had said. He wasn't afraid of anything.

Ben crept back to the west side of the landing, where he had last seen Tom. But how can I get into that cocoon without alerting Tom, Ben thought? I need to figure something out and fast. If I shimmy down the rope it will alert Tom and he might kill Eva, Ben reasoned. If I jumped down on the canvas I might slide off. But I've got to do something. While looking over the side he saw the ambulance arrive.

He didn't want Tom to know he was on the landing so he had to keep hidden. Ben's father had lost his life trying to save a fellow logger. Now Ben knew he was going to have to risk his life to save Eva. This would be where he would overcome all the humiliation he had suffered in his life. Ben knew he was ready to risk everything to save his beloved's life. Then he heard the wind increase, knocking the platform against the concrete. The platform shuddered. Another gale pushed the platform even harder, ripping off canvas that had concealed Tom. Ben saw Tom looking down with his revolver in his hand.

"Don't come up here! I'll push Eva over the side," he bellowed. Ben watched as Tom lifted Eva's limp body and draped it on the rail of the platform. Tom shot at the men below. The sight of Eva's lifeless body hanging there fired Ben's outrage. He imagined his father carrying an unconscious man from the path of certain death, and realized that if he didn't act now, Eva's death was all but certain. In his anguish Ben leapt over the rail. He plunged downward, twenty-five feet.

Tom looked up in alarm and made a feeble effort to raise his gun before Ben crashed down on him.

Ben shoved Tom's head against the boards and slammed it down onto a bag of concrete. Ben's adrenaline was out of control and he smashed his fist into the Tom's mouth.

Realizing that Tom was out of action or even dead, Ben turned to Eva. Another blast of wind shook the scaffolding. She was barely breathing. He pulled her off the platform fence and gently laid her on the wooden floor. Then he untied the pulley ropes and lowered the rigging to the base of the tower. Ben lifted Eva over the rail and into the arms of Officer Stout who had climbed a ladder to the scaffolding. He carried her carefully, down the ladder. Waiting on the ground were two nurses with a stretcher. Then all three carried her to the waiting ambulance. The doctor inside helped the nurses place Eva on a cot. Officer Stout closed the ambulance's doors.

The ambulance's siren blared as they rushed Eva to Astoria's hospital. Officer Stout rushed back to the ladder and climbed up to the scaffolding. "Where's Tom?"

"Over there," Ben pointed.

Officer Stout checked Tom's pulse. Then he put his ear to Tom's mouth to see if he could hear breathing. "Tom's dead," he said. He picked up Tom's gun and held it in his hand as he climbed back down the ladder to his police car.

Ben climbed down too. He went over to the officer's car.

"The coroner is on his way to pick up Tom's body." Officer Stout said through his window. "That was a fool thing you did. You could've been killed. Next time let the police do the dirty work, understand!"

"Yes, sir," Ben said. "What about Eva?"

"She's in good hands now," Officer Stout said. "Follow me and I'll show you the way to the hospital."

"By the way, why is that scaffolding hanging up there anyway?" Ben asked.

"That's an artist's platform," Stout said. "Designed by a black fellow, Attilio Pusterla. He's in charge of making the mural that will wrap around the tower from the top to the bottom. Historical pictures, from what I understand. He's a genius at designing murals."

"I'll have to come back to see it when it's finished," Ben said. "But now, I'll follow you to the hospital."

Chapter Forty-two

At the hospital Ben waited in the visitor's room for about an hour. While he waited a nurse came in and cleaned his head wound. Then she wrapped a bandage over the bruise. Just after the nurse left, a doctor came through the double doors.

"Hi, my name is Doctor Barnes. You must be Ben Cooper."

"Yes, I am." Ben shook his hand.

"Miss Barton is in room 214. She's still unconscious. I'm afraid I can't promise she'll ever wake up, Mr. Cooper. During her captivity she was forced to take a big dose of morphine. All we can do now is wait and hope she recovers. You may sit in her room if you wish."

"Just show me the way," Ben said.

"Come with me."

Ben followed the doctor up a stairwell to the second floor. The doctor led him to her room and opened the door. Ben walked inside. She was lying under white sheets, barely breathing, with one bare arm draped across her body. The room was stark white and had two gray night stands on either side of the bed. On one stand was a black telephone and on the other was a glass and pitcher. At the foot of the bed was another stand with a clipboard on it. A colorful painting of a Columbia River Gorge sunset hung above Eva's bed. The picture helped to soften the sterile coldness of the room.

Ben put his hand caressingly on Eva's forehead

and cheek. He bent down and kissed her gently on the nose. The doctor brought a chair for Ben. Diffused sunlight came in through the window's curtains.

"Please let me know immediately if she wakes," Doctor Barnes said. "Is there anything else I can do?"

"Yes, I need to use the phone," Ben said.

"Just tell the operator the number you want and she'll connect you. I have other patients to attend to but I'll check in later to see how she's doing."

"Could I get a typewriter and few more chairs?" Ben asked.

"A typewriter?" the doctor asked. "Why?"

"I'm a newspaper reporter."

"I see. All right then, I'll have one sent up."

Ben picked up the telephone and asked the operator to connect him with the Toledo Spruce mill in Toledo.

"Mother, this is Ben. I just wanted you to know what happened."

After Ben told his mother about his harrowing trip to Astoria, she said, "I'll be there as soon as I can."

Next Ben called Eva's father, and then he called his editor. Both of them said they would begin preparations for the drive to Astoria.

A nurse's aide in a colorful red-and-white uniform came in carrying a typewriter. She set it on a desk against the wall.

"Wow! That was heavy," she said with a smile. "How many chairs will you need?"

"Three more. Thank you," Ben said. Within a few minutes the aide brought the other chairs. Then she closed the door behind her.

Ben had begun to notice that Eva's complexion was slowly changing. The color in her face was returning. Her breathing seemed to be getting stronger. Or maybe it was just wishful thinking. But since he planned on staying, he decided he might as well start writing his article on the Roosevelt Highway. He could give it to Jess when he arrived.

Ben worked on his story for most of the day. The clacking of the typewriter didn't seem to faze Eva, so he just kept on working. Every once in a while he would get up and check her. He thought she seemed to be improving. At five p.m. he finally finished his article. Then he went back to his bedside position and dozed off, his chin slumping onto his chest.

His mother woke him up by shaking his shoulder. "Hello there."

'Mother?" Ben cleared his head and stood up. "I'm glad you're here." He embraced her.

"What happened to your head?" Rosa asked.

"I took a nasty blow from the butt of Tom's revolver. Would you help me take this bandage off?"

Rosa carefully took the bandage off. "There, that should feel better," Rosa said then looked at Eva. "Poor dear, I talked with Dr. Evans on the way up. His assessment was much worse than what I'm seeing here. She must be regaining her strength."

"I thought so, too," Ben said.

Rosa put her hand on Eva's forehead. "She doesn't have a temperature and she has good color. I've seen a lot of sick people but this woman is recovering."

Fifteen minutes later, Doctor Evans came through the door. He picked up the clipboard at the foot of the bed, looked it over, and then walked to the opposite side of the bed. He felt Eva's forehead and picked up her limp wrist to check Eva's pulse.

"Well, well, well. Her pulse is considerably stronger then a few hours ago. Looks like she might wake up pretty soon. She's definitely out of danger." Then he put the clipboard back on the stand and left the room.

There was a knock on the door. Ben got up and opened it. Jess walked in. "I can't stay long, I wanted to check in to see how Eva was."

"I'm glad you could come," Ben said. Jess sat in the chair across from Ben and his mother.

The next person to arrive was Andrew Barton. Before Ben could say a word, he was at his daughter's side, kissing her forehead. "Please wake up my darling child." Andrew brushed away a tear. "What's the prognosis," he asked Ben?

"The doctor came though a while back and was amazed at her progress," Ben said. "Things looked grim this morning, but all of us agree that her color has returned and her pulse is significantly more pronounced. The doctor said she was out of danger."

"Thank heavens," Andrew sat down next to his friend Jess.

They sat there most of the night, the four of them dozing off now and then, but always vigilant on the status of Eva.

Early the next morning Jess announced that he had to leave. "Ben, I must get back to the paper, but before I go I'd like to talk with you in the hall."

"Yes, sir." Ben followed Jess through the door.

"I know this is a bad time to ask, Ben, but did you write that story about the Roosevelt Highway?"

Ben had carried the typed manuscript with him. "Here it is. I worked on it all day while sitting with Eva. I've also done a lot of thinking while cooped up here, and I have other news to tell you."

"What is it?" Jess said.

"I've decided to quit the newspaper business."

"You've got to be kidding," Jess said. "Listen, you've been under a lot of strain with this episode on the Coast. Good jobs are hard to find, and you're one of my best writers. I'll tell you what, how about if I give you a promotion? I've been thinking about it anyway, and you've sure earned it."

"Thank you, sir. But I've decided to help Eva and her father by writing freelance articles. I'll be writing about the Coast Range Forests and how they're being destroyed."

"Well, if that's what you want," Jess said. "I'd be interested in reviewing and publishing your work."

"When Eva recovers, I'll start sending you our work. I've learned a lot on this trip up the Coast. It's hard for a woman writer to be taken seriously. No one believed Eva when she told them about almost being raped."

"A sad ordeal," Jess said.

"Because the police didn't believe her, a lunatic wound up chasing us up the Coast, trying to kill us at every turn. With the same kind of honesty, Eva has been trying to tell people about the rape of the Coast Range forests. Years from now there won't be any old trees. The vegetation and animal life that they protect will vanish too. I've changed my mind because of what Eva has taught me. With my own eyes, I've seen that she's speaking the truth. Money is the corrupting influence. Now I feel it's my mission to help her explain what's really happening to our Oregon forests."

"I understand only too well," Jess said. "Your message is years ahead of its time. Please give my best to Eva when she wakes." The two men shook hands. Ben watched as Jess's head bobbed down the stairwell and out of sight.

Back in Eva's room three people sat solemnly.

"Mr. Barton, I want you to know that I've proposed to Eva."

"What, you've proposed to my daughter?" Andrew raised his eyebrows.

"Yes, sir. And she accepted me."

"Well! This certainly throws a new slant on all our lives," Andrew said.

"What do you mean?"

"I recently received a large inheritance—more money then I thought possible. I want to use that money to buy a large tract of virgin forest land in the Coast Range," Andrew said.

Just then Eva's eyes opened. She blinked.

"Eva! You're awake!" Ben quickly knelt by her side. Then he turned to his mother "Go get the doctor, hurry."

Rosa rushed out of the room.

"I feel awful," Eva whispered. She put her shaking hand to her head.

"The doctor will be here shortly," Ben said. "Just relax for now. You're at the Astoria hospital."

"Oh Ben, I was so scared. Where's Tom?"

"Tom will never bother you again. The police have taken him away."

"Father, is this true?"

"Yes honey, it's true."

"Ben has proposed to me and I accepted." Eva looked at Ben. "Or was that just a dream?"

"No, that's all true, Eva," Ben said, smiling. "I just told your father about it."

"Yes," Andrew said. "I wish you both all the best."

The doctor hurried in the door with a small cup in his hand. He went immediately to Eva. "Drink this and you'll feel better." He helped her drink the medicine.

After drinking, Eva fell back to sleep and slept for the rest of the day. She woke up at six p.m., very hungry. She was brought a tray of food and she devoured it. Then she propped herself up on her pillow, wanting to join in on the talk about the family's future.

"It's a miracle Tom didn't kill you with that

overdose of morphine," Andrew said.

"That's in the past father," Eva said. "Let's talk about the future, okay?"

"Certainly," Andrew said. "I was telling Ben that I just came into a large inheritance from your great aunt in New England. I've got some ideas on how I'd like to use it."

"I'm listening," Eva said.

"Now that I know you two are engaged to be married, I think my plans for the inheritance make even more sense. I'd like to save a large section of Coast Range forest for posterity. I know of some acreage for sale on the Wilson River, northeast of Tillamook. It's prime forestland. Our family will be stewards, researching every aspect of what constitutes a forest."

"Ben, that's forestland like the one that we camped in, do you remember?"

"How could I forget?" Ben replied.

"You and Ben can continue your writings about saving Oregon's forests," Andrew continued. "We can contact other conservation groups to get ideas on how we can set up our own Oregon organization. Are you kids ready for an adventure like that? "

"Father, would you help us build a log cabin?"

"Sure I will, sugar," Andrew said.

"We'll be able to grow our own produce for canning to last through the winters," Ben said.

"I'd like to help too," Rosa said.

Ben put his arm around his mother's shoulder and hugged her. "That makes it unanimous."

THE END

About the Author

Since his retirement in 1997 as a public safety officer at the University of Oregon, Joe Blakely has authored fve books and several articles. His books include: *The Bellfountain Giant Killers,* the story of a small Oregon high school that won the 1937 state basketball championship against seemingly impossible odds,

The Tall Firs, an account of the University of Oregon winnning the first NCAA basketball championship in 1939, *The Heirloom,* an historical novel set in Bandon, Oreogn in 1920, *Lifting Oregon Out of the Mud,* a story about building the Oregon Coast Highway through 1936, and now a new historical noval, *Kidnapped,* that takes

Photo by Pauline Rughani

place along the Oregon Coast Highway in 1926. In 2003, his article *The Nestle Condensary in Bandon* was published in the <u>Oregon Historical Quarterly</u> magazine.

Mr. Blakely is currently marketing a screenplay based on *The Bellfountain Giant Killers.*

Order Form

Autographed copies of this or Joe Blakely's other four books may be ordered from the author.

COPIES	TITLE	PRICE	TOTAL
_____	Kidnapped...on Oregon's Coast Highway	$15.00	_____
_____	The Heirloom. A novel set in Bandon Oregon (1920)	$15.00	_____
_____	The Tall Firs: The Story of the University of Oregon and The First NCAA Basketball Championship	$10.00	_____
_____	The Bellfountain Giant Killers, the Story of a Small Oregon High School and its Miraculous Championship Season	$10.00	_____
_____	Lifting Oregon Out of the Mud, Building the Oregon Coast Highway	$15.00	_____

Please include $3.00 shipping and handling for one book, and $2.00 for each additional book. Payment must accompany orders. Allow 3 weeks for delivery.

My check or money order is enclosed for $_____ .

Name _____

Organization _____

Address _____

City/State/Zip _____

Phone _____ Email _____

Make check payable to:

Joe R. Blakely

P.O. Box 40113

Eugene Oregon 97404

Order Form

Autographed copies of this or Joe Blakely's other four books may be ordered from the author.

COPIES	TITLE	PRICE	TOTAL
_____	Kidnapped...on Oregon's Coast Highway	$15.00	_____
_____	The Heirloom. A novel set in Bandon Oregon (1920)	$15.00	_____
_____	The Tall Firs: The Story of the University of Oregon and The First NCAA Basketball Championship	$10.00	_____
_____	The Bellfountain Giant Killers, the Story of a Small Oregon High School and its Miraculous Championship Season	$10.00	_____
_____	Lifting Oregon Out of the Mud, Building the Oregon Coast Highway	$15.00	_____

Please include $3.00 shipping and handling for one book, and $2.00 for each additional book. Payment must accompany orders. Allow 3 weeks for delivery.

My check or money order is enclosed for $_____ .

Name _____

Organization _____

Address _____

City/State/Zip _____

Phone _____ Email _____

Make check payable to:

Joe R. Blakely

P.O. Box 40113

Eugene Oregon 97404